48 Clues
into the
Disappearance
of My Sister

Joyce Carol Oates, literary icon, is the author of
more than 70 books, including novels, short story
collections, poetry, plays, essays, and criticism,
and the winner of a host of prizes including
the National Book Award and a Guggenheim
Fellowship. Oates is Professor of the Humanities
at Princeton University.

Follow Joyce on @JoyceCarolOates

Also by Joyce Carol Oates

The Barrens

Beasts

Cardiff, by the Sea: Four Novellas

The Corn Maiden and Other Nightmares

Daddy Love

Dis Mem Ber and Other Stories of Mystery and Suspense

The Doll-Master and Other Tales of Terror

Evil Eye: Four Novellas of Love Gone Wrong

Extenuating Circumstances

A Fair Maiden

The Female of the Species: Tales of Mystery and Suspense

Give Me Your Heart: Tales of Mystery and Suspense

High Crime Area: Tales of Darkness and Dread

Jack of Spades: A Tale of Suspense

The Museum of Dr. Moses: Tales of Mystery and Suspense

Night, Neon

Night-Gaunts and Other Tales of Suspense

Pursuit: A Tale of Suspense

Rape: A Love Story

48 Clues into the Disappearance of My Sister

JOYCE CAROL OATES

An Apollo Book

First published in the US in 2023 by Mysterious Press,
an imprint of Penzler Publishers

First published in the UK in 2023 by Head of Zeus Ltd,
part of Bloomsbury Publishing Plc

9 7 5 3 1 2 4 6 8

A catalogue record for this book is available from the British Library.

ISBN (HB): 9781837932771
ISBN (XTPB): 9781837932788
ISBN (E): 9781837932757

Interior Design by Maria Fernandez

Printed and bound in Great Britain by
CPI Group (UK) Ltd, Croydon CR0 4YY

Head of Zeus Ltd
5–8 Hardwick Street
London EC1R 4RG

WWW.HEADOFZEUS.COM

for Otto Penzler

PART I

1

Silky White Fabric, Bodiless. Pool of silk, in languid-liquidy folds on the floor where (the viewer/voyeur avidly assumes) she'd shrugged her naked body out of the shift, let it fall slithering like a snake, but a sheerly white, purely white, camellia-white silky snake falling past her hips, her thighs and to the carpeted floor in a hiss.

Though bodiless, boneless, smelling faintly, fragrantly of a (female) body.

◆

Is that a clue? The flimsy white silk Dior "slip dress" belonging to my sister M. discovered on the floor of her bedroom.

3

Subsequent to her disappearance on April 11, 1991.

Or: is the article of clothing of little significance, purely chance, irrelevant and accidental, *not* a clue?

◆

(In a later time in history, certainly in the 21st century, M.'s silky white slip dress would have been examined for DNA; particularly the scummy clue called *semen*. But in 1991 in small-town upstate Aurora-on-Cayuga, New York forensic science was little known, and so the chic silk Dior with the spaghetti straps, neatly hung on a hanger in M.'s closet, by me, the protective younger sister, has awaited M.'s return all these years undefiled.)

◆

(Though yes, possibly the silk dress on the floor of M.'s bedroom was a "clue"—if we'd known if the dress had been purchased by M. herself during her three-year sojourn in New York City or if it was gift from a lover and, if so, which lover.)

(Also, a clue in that it had been dropped in haste, or negligently, by M. who was ordinarily so fastidious she would never have allowed an article of clothing to fall to

4

the floor and not retrieve it immediately, hanging it in a closet, or folding and putting it neatly into a drawer. For Marguerite Fulmer was *cool, calm, control.* A self-styled sculptor: one who *shapes*, but is not *shaped*.)

(Letting clothes fall onto the floor of her room, accumulating over days, weeks, refusing to allow the housekeeper into her room was more characteristic of M.'s "difficult" younger sister G. but since G. had not ever gone missing from Aurora-on-Cayuga no one gave a damn about the condition of G.'s room, or took the time, in twenty-two years, to search it.)

◆

Silky white fabric, bodiless. Shimmering, slithering down the woman's hips, the ivory-pale (naked) body, exposing that body with a *shhhing* sound like a snake's hiss. Staring you do not wish to stare, it is demeaning to stare, too much pride and self-respect to stare, indeed *you do not stare* and yet (helplessly) you observe the flimsy slip dress fall to the floor, a pool at the woman's ivory-pale (naked) feet.

5

2

Double Mirror. The means by which I saw my sister on the morning of the day she was to "disappear" from our lives.

That is, the means by which I happened to see M.'s reflection in a mirror for (in fact) I did not see Marguerite herself, only her reflection.

(It is imprecise, if common, to say that the [reflected] image is the person; but, in this instance, the reflection of M. was but a reflection of the [unknowable, inscrutable] M., in fact *the reflection of a reflection.*)

Mornings begin early at our house. In winter, before dawn we are likely to be awake if not fully dressed.

But then, it was April. Yet a chill wintry dawn like a celestial eye slowly—grudgingly—opening to fill the leaden sky.

Passing by M.'s room on my way downstairs, surprised that her door eased open as if by a draft, for usually M.'s door was shut firmly against unwanted intrusions and cheery morning greetings, I could not resist glancing inside, and so happened to see, in the vertical mirror attached to the inside of my sister's closet door, which was also partially open, about six feet away, the reflection of M. on the farther side of the room, facing her bureau mirror; so that, wholly unpremeditatedly, in the suddenness of the moment, my eyes took in, without accessing, scarcely registering, my sister's wraithlike face in the bureau mirror reflected in the mirror on the closet door—that is, an image *double mirrored*.

All this, vertiginously recalled (now) twenty-two years later as one might recall a dream of utter mystery that, in the intervening years, has not lightened in mystery but deepened.

(Possibly, in the periphery of my eye I "saw" the Dior dress on the floor. But such "seeing" was not conscious at the time and if it seems conscious in retrospect, that is the mind playing its mischievous and perverse tricks upon itself.)

(No, I *did not see* the flimsy white dress sliding down my sister's naked body to lie like a shimmering pool of white at her feet. I am sure that I *did not see this* though it seems that I remember it vividly.)

What I do remember clearly: my (beautiful) (doomed) sister standing with her back to me on the farther side of the room as she was brushing her long straight silvery-blond hair, reflected in the vertical mirror upon which my eyes fixed in a sort of startled fascination even as the thought came to me *No, this is forbidden!*—gazing with dread upon my sister as if I were, not an adult woman in her mid-twenties, a woman with a definite, one might say *indelibly* formed personality, but a pubescent child; for years in awe of the (aloof, elegant) sister six years older than I.

Peering through a doorway into the interior of another's life: the apprehension that we will glimpse the other, the sister, in a state of unwanted intimacy, nakedness.

Was M. naked, standing before the bureau mirror reflected in the closet mirror? The pale straight back, perfectly shaped waist, hips, thighs, legs.

Shadowy vertebrae, slender wrists, ankles.

(Of course) in reporting this (fleeting/involuntary) glance into M.'s room to detectives I would say nothing about what M. was wearing. If one of them had thought to ask me—(no one ever did)—I would have said with a frown *Oh I don't know, a bathrobe, I suppose, what would you think?*

Nothing annoys me so much as pests poking their noses into my private life.

8

My father's private life, and mine. Keep your damned distance!

No doubt by this time M. had showered in her anti-quated, barely serviceable shower and taken time to shampoo her long showy hair as (I had reason to think) she did several times a week out of vanity, pride in herself and her beauty, which was the sort of "classic" beauty that pretends to be unaware of itself.

In contrast to me, the younger sister G., with a legiti-mate reason to wish to be unaware of her appearance, who often didn't trouble to wash her hair for weeks.

M., brandishing a gilt-backed brush that had once belonged to our mother, brushing her hair in long lan-guorous strokes causing hairs to crackle with static electricity.

Yes, I'd noticed *that*. A *frisson* of static electricity that caused the hairs on my arms to rise in sympathy.

Strange how M. was oblivious of me. *Oblivious of what was rushing at her from the future on wide-spread dark-feathered wings.*

Almost, I wanted to call to her: "Hi there! Hel-*lo*."

Almost, I might have warned her: "Marguerite! Take care!"

If I'd called to her would M. have peered at me in the mirror(s), or would M. have turned a startled face to me?

9

I will never know. For I dared not speak.

To this day the phenomenon of the *double mirror* remains a mystery: of *little consequence, purely accidental* in the exigency of the moment, and yet *essential*. For, though the fleetingly aligned mirrors were necessary in order that, for the final time, I would see my sister, the *double mirror* was the only means by which I could have seen her, since the door to her room would have blocked my view of her in front of the bureau, under ordinary circumstances.

By chance then, a draft of cold air in the second-floor corridor must have blown the door open, which was not uncommon in our old drafty house.

(A nuisance that I'd learned to prevent by securing my door when I was inside my room: pushing a heavy stack of books against the door at the bottom.)

M.'s "room"—(as it was called)—wasn't a singular room but three adjoining rooms running the length of the eastern side of the house and overlooking, at a distance of about one hundred feet, the choppy waves of Cayuga Lake, the largest of the "scenic" Finger Lakes.

My own room, which *was* a single room, was on the other side of the corridor, adjacent but not (of course) connected with the master bedroom, a large suite of rooms taking up the remainder of the second floor.

(Father's room, this was. Which I never, or rarely, entered. Then, only if invited. Once the master bedroom had been beautifully furnished by our mother and may have become, in intervening years, somewhat shabby or careworn, inhabited just by Father, and then reluctantly for Father preferred to spend much of his time at his office in downtown Aurora or in his home office here in the house, on the first floor, rear.)

Making my way along the corridor scarcely hesitating at M.'s (part-opened) door as if this were, not a cataclysmic day in the life of our family, perhaps even (in retrospect) a defining day, but a totally ordinary day, headed for the front staircase with its hardwood banister and wide steps covered in a worn maroon plush carpeting, so unlike the narrower, thinly carpeted back stairs of the massive old seven-bedroom, five-bathroom English Tudor on Cayuga Avenue; making my way like a sleepwalker under the spell (as I could not have known, yet) of the *double mirror* that would haunt me for decades. Not sinister, but rather neutral, as a pane of glass is neutral, regardless of what we are forced to see through it, M.'s mirrors, precisely because they were so accidentally aligned, and so fleetingly, may have suggested, to me, a premonitory aura of the unreal, the unsubstantiated, even the phantasmagoric, imposed upon what was but an ordinary domestic scene: a resident of the house passing by the doorway of an older sister on her way downstairs to breakfast at about 7:20 A.M. at the outset of what should have been just one in a sequence of mostly unremarked, ordinary days in April 1991.

Which leaves the matter ambiguous: was the *double mirror* the means by which I "saw" into a profound and inexplicable mystery, or was the *double mirror* the profound and inexplicable mystery itself?

3

Missing Person. It would be claimed that M. "stepped off the face of the earth"—"vanished into thin air"—"disappeared without a trace."

Was this true? *Is* it?

For no one is truly *missing*. Everyone is *somewhere* though we may not know where.

Even the dead—their remains. *Somewhere.*

It is well known in Aurora how Father is still hopeful. And I, the younger sister, the *less beautiful, less talented sister* will express "hope" if queried.

"Yes! Every hour of every day I grind my teeth in dismay, despair, resentment, fury. *My sister is not 'missing'— my sister is* somewhere."

And, I have been known to say, earnestly: "In hiding, maybe. Or in disguise. Just to spite us. To spite *me*."

After a moment adding: "Even if Marguerite is no longer living still she has got to be *somewhere*."

If only the slender bones. Swath of pale silvery-blond hair that fell seductively past her shoulders.

The remains of the pearly-perfect teeth, maybe. That final grimace out of hard-packed black earth looking like triumph.

4

Early Spring. In upstate New York spring is slow to emerge out of winter as a steaming breath out of a cavernous mouth.

Exactly when M. left the house is not known. *I* did not see her leave nor did Father (as we would report to detectives). Our housekeeper Lena did not see her. Presumably after 7:20 A.M. But probably no later than 8 A.M. For it was M.'s routine to walk/hike to the college and it was rare that she arrived there, if she was going there at all, after 9 A.M.

A thinly overcast morning. Thursday: the very epitome of a *nothing-day*.

Dripping icicles from the eaves of our house, ice-toothed sludge underfoot, northern sides of yews serrated with frost slow to melt. Is this what M. noticed, or was M. thinking of something very different?

Was M. thinking *guiltily* of something very different?

Aurora-on-Cayuga is built on a half-dozen hills overlooking a lake and so it is always at the whim of the "lake effect"—rapidly shifting weather, piercing sun through clouds, a possibility of spitting rain.

This seems to be definite: M. was wearing her ankle-high mahogany-dark Ferragamo leather boots with a low but distinctive heel. Her footprints led through the tall yews behind our house in the direction of the narrow asphalt road that within a half mile bifurcated the steeply hilly "historic" campus of Aurora College for Women, founded 1878: a cluster of austere old red-brick buildings with grim weatherworn facades, South Hall, Minor Hall, Wells Hall, Fulmer Hall adjoining the newly built Cayuga Arts School where M. was "junior artist-in-residence" and taught a class in sculpting.

M.'s boot prints, leading from the rear door of our house through the trampled grass of our back lawn stretching for an acre then passing out of our property and into the no-man's-land of winter-damaged deciduous trees and underbrush that belonged to Cayuga County, soon lost amid myriad footprints and animal tracks on the path winding through the woods to Drumlin Road.

If we'd known. If we'd realized she would never return. Photographing the Ferragamo prints. Determining if the prints continued on the farther side of Drumlin Road or if by that time they had vanished, which could only mean that someone (unknown) had stopped for M. on the road, forced her into his vehicle or (perhaps) M. had climbed into the vehicle of her own volition calling softly to the driver, "Here I am."

5

Last Seen. How many times asked: when did you see your sister last? And what did you say to each other?

And very carefully I would explain that I'd last seen my sister at about 7:20 A.M. on the morning of her "disappearance" but we had not exchanged words.

I had seen *her*; she had not seen *me*.

And the fools would persist asking when had I spoken with my sister last, and what had she said. And I would make every effort to remember, and to answer sincerely.

Saying *Marguerite did not say anything to me to indicate that she was unhappy or anxious or worried.* Not saying *We did not have that kind of relationship! We were not sisters who confided in each other, especially Marguerite did not confide in me about her lovers. You are very naive to assume so.*

Nor did I tell them that to be precise I'd seen, not my sister, but the reflection of my sister in the *double mirror*.

And not M.'s face, not clearly. For M.'s face was framed in the bureau mirror, a blurred oval as if partially erased. Scarcely recognizable, if I hadn't known it was her. The beauty, and the blemishes in the beauty.

For mirrors double distances and make of the familiar, strangeness.

6

Revenge. There is a famous/notorious work of art, a drawing by Willem de Kooning "erased" by Robert Rauschenberg in 1953. You could say that the lesser artist revenges himself upon the greater artist by erasing his work. A playful sort of vandalism that might be mistaken for whimsy.

For what other revenge can the lesser artist achieve, than erasing work by the greater artist?

I was not an artist. M. had no fear of me erasing her work.

I *was* a poet. But my poems were secrets scribbled in code for mice scrambling in my desk drawers to peruse.

The spell M. cast upon all who knew her: our parents ·most of all.

Her beauty, that was unjust. For all beauty is unjust. Her kindness, that seemed (to me) an expression of vanity. Her softness of heart, when she dared remove her armor. Her (apparent) love for *me*. Or, affection for me.

As if I were, not a rival of M.'s, no one to take seriously, the awkward younger sister, a slightly unkempt sheepdog, burly, bumbling, bulgy-damp-eyed, with a big moist nose, pink tongue panting, quickly out of breath from the stairs.

Even my name, G.—"Georgene"—so much less beautiful than "Marguerite."

Named for an obscure aunt of my mother's. Married, kept house in a prestigious neighborhood in Aurora, had servants, had children, passed into oblivion—a total cipher. The insult!

It was said—it was claimed—that M. had moved back home from New York City for my sake after Mother's death. That M. "gave up her Guggenheim year"—as if she'd have had to return the money if she returned to Aurora. (I know for a fact that M. *did not return the Guggenheim grant.*)

Among the relatives, in particular our callow catty girl-cousins, it has been said that my sister returned to Aurora to "save" me when (it seemed) I was *suicidal.*

(Which is absurd: I do not "believe" in suicide any more than, for instance, Father would believe in suicide, which, to him, as to his Teutonic-warrior *Volkmar* ancestors, would be *giving God-damned solace to the enemy*.)

Why I hated M., if I'd hated her, which (I am sure) I did not.

For *why* would I hate my sister who took pity on me, when she took notice of me, when she had time for me. *Why* hate my sister who was (said to be) the only person who cared for me enough to care for me, for Christ's sake. After Mother's death which was a misty-crappy-smelly-bog time inaccessible to (my) memory.

Fun times! Overseeing the vacuuming, cleaning, scouring, airing-out of my pigsty-room from which poor despairing Lena had been banished for a full year, and Father himself, the Zeus of our household, had not the courage or fortitude to enter.

Pressing on me her fancy French lavender soap, a "bribe" for me to shower more often.

Plaiting my thick "obstinate" hair, as she'd called it. A promise of a birthday excursion to Niagara Falls—"just the two of us, Gigi . . ."

Gigi!—M.'s secret name for me, that no one knew.

Gigi!—a sensation rises in me like delirium, the impulse is to shout, laugh wildly, scream, and it is hateful, so many years later when such folly should be laid to rest. Someone should shove dirt into my mouth, to quiet me.

Of course, some of the things M. passed on to me, so suitable for her, fitting her slender body, were too small for me, or in some way inappropriate. Which (surely) M. knew.

A lavender suede handbag, ruined in the rain the first time I used it. (But had G. *known?* That rain is injurious to expensive suede? No? Yes?)

Is it possible, though not very *likely*, that my sister would have passed on to me the Ferragamo boots she'd bought in New York City?—a cruel joke since Gigi with her size-ten feet couldn't possibly have worn the elegant size-seven boots.

Yes but *maybe* there is a diabolical scenario in which the calculating Gigi, wielding the boots in question, ingeniously managed to create boot-tracks leading from the rear of our house into the no-man's-land where the tracks became "lost" in a welter of other tracks.

(But when could Gigi have possibly done this? Not on the morning of April 11, 1991, surely.)

Possibly the previous night. Undetected.

For no one (except the younger sister) reported having seen M. that morning.

And so, perhaps it isn't accurate to say that M. was wearing the Ferragamo boots that morning but rather that, as detectives duly noted, *boot prints were clearly discernible* leading from the back door / back steps of the house,

23

through the winter-roughened lawn, and to the adjoining township property, where they commingled with other prints and were lost.

So many *maybes*! Yet (this is the tantalizing promise of clues!) one of these *maybes* however improbable and implausible is the Truth.

7

April 11, 1991. On her calendar for this day M. had noted, in pencil, just two routine items: 2 P.M. (class), 5 P.M. (committee meeting).

And the following day, dentist's appointment at 9 A.M.

Following week, more of the same: routine appointments, meetings, conferences with students. Banality/security of daily life. Nothing of significance an investigator might decode as a *clue*.

Unless the calendar for April was carefully planned by M. To deceive with very ordinariness.

◆

Weekdays it was M.'s custom to arrive early in the morning at the Arts School to work in her studio undisturbed through the morning and so when M. failed to arrive by noon her (apparent) absence began to be noted in the Art Department though not (yet) particularly remarked upon, until 2 P.M. when students arrived for the sculpting class, M.'s absence now acknowledged and calls to M.'s phone unanswered; queries began to be made—*Have you seen Marguerite today? Have you spoken with Marguerite today?*

Not yet alarm, of course. Affable, quizzical: *Has anyone seen Marguerite this morning? No?*

Note: the name "Marguerite" is uttered with a certain reverence. Admiring, not accusatory.

Mar-guer-ite: the full, melodic name, not a vulgar rush of syllables.

An hour later growing curiosity where M. might be, why M. hadn't called or sent a note, definitely wasn't in her studio, nowhere in the arts building, no messages.

And still not (yet) alarm, no actual concern that M. might have met with a mishap, might be ill, derailed by an emergency, in any sort of distress.

Very possibly, there was a "family crisis" at the Fulmer residence—for it was known, not generally, but by some, that M.'s younger sister G. had "some sort of history. . . ."

What kind of history? Mental—?

26

. . . hospitalized? In Buffalo?

Only cautiously were such possibilities mentioned for M. was known to be a *very private person* who did not speak casually of her family life; unlike her artist-colleagues who gossiped shamelessly, joked openly and cruelly of their difficult/comical families presented for the ribald consumption of others like comic strips on a bulletin board.

Very private, too, about the men in her life. Not clear if indeed there was a man in M.'s life at the time of her disappearance.

Unless the silky Dior slip dress was a clue: not "fragrant" (possibly) but "smelly" with the unmistakable smell of a man. . . .

But no one will know: no strangers will invade M.'s private quarters staring rudely and suspiciously at the "evidence" the missing person has left behind for discreetly I will pick up the wisp of a dress which M. has unaccountably left lying on the floor, an article of clothing light as lingerie, and I will hang it on a hanger, and place it (inconspicuously) at the very rear of M.'s closet, where no prying detectives are likely to find it.

For though I did not approve of M.'s (possible, probable) sexually promiscuous life, kept entirely secret from me, I did care, very much, about the *good name* of the Fulmer

27

family which dates back to the time of the earliest settlers in this part of New York State: 1789.

Indeed, there is a Fulmer County east of here, near Albany, where the first Fulmers settled; a branch of the family long broken off from our own, and of no interest to us.

◆

Through the afternoon of April 11 calls began to come to M.'s private line at our house, which rang only in M.'s room, and which Lena did not answer, by M.'s request; these were calls from M.'s colleagues and friends at the Arts School, wondering where she was.

Messages were left. In all, eight messages from "concerned" friends and one annoyingly "urgent" message from the (male) colleague who was the senior artist-in-residence at the college.

In fact, there was a second "urgent" message from this individual, a particularly self-aggrandizing pseudo-*artiste* who called himself "Elke," whose interest in M. was proprietary and offensive. (More of insufferable "Elke," later.)

(And where was I during these hours, I would be asked by detectives, happy to inform the fools that I was *at my place of work*, where would they think?—a steady stream of customers at the Mill Street Post Office, plus my two co-workers at the counter, and our supervisor, all could and did testify to my *whereabouts* that day.)

(So ridiculous! *Whereabouts, alibis—clues.* Clichés of the police investigation banal and threadbare as a worn old carpet over which, nonetheless, one has to trudge, eyes straight ahead in a pose of lockjaw-deadpan innocence.)

Oblivious of the flurry of concern for M.'s whereabouts I continued to work until 5 P.M. at the Mill Street P.O. No shiver of premonition or apprehension!—none.

Departing then to walk home as usual. Or you might say *trudge*—eyes averted from fellow pedestrians, down-looking, frowning, sending out signals as a bat sends out radar—*No cheery hellos or how-are-yous thanking you beforehand.*

Also, unlike M. I did not own a car. I did not have a license to drive granted by the State of New York to some citizens while withheld arbitrarily from others.

Arriving at home in time to hear the phone ringing in M.'s room as I ascended the stairs to the second floor. Several calls, or the same party calling persistently, very annoying to me, for after a long day at the post office waiting on idiots with poorly taped packages to send parcel post my nerves are easily jangled, and so I dared to enter M.'s room in her (presumed) absence to answer

29

the damned phone in a voice making no effort to be polite: "Yes? Hello? If you're looking for who I think you are, sorry she isn't here."

Why such concern in the silly woman's voice, who was this person to pretend to be concerned for *my* sister, couldn't help but interrupt her in my blunt no-bullshit way, and silly Sally or whatever her name was was shocked, and said, stammering: "But—where *is* Marguerite? Are you the sister? Aren't you worried? This is not like Marguerite, to miss her sculpture class without giving any . . ."

"And how do you know what my sister is 'like'?"— couldn't resist, the caller was no one I knew. Hysterical like a hen with its head cut off if the decapitated head could chitter and chatter. "She could be in Timbuktu by now, what's it to *you*?"

Hanging up then, laughing. And a few minutes later the phone rang again, and again I answered it: "Sor-ree wrong number. Good*byee*."

Giving my voice a sort of Chinese inflection. Had to laugh.

For they were *all so silly*. When there was no cause for alarm, *not an emergency situation at all*.

Gave a quick perusal of M.'s quarters including her bedroom (bed: neatly made, coverlet in place, even on all sides) and bathroom (towels neatly hung on racks).

Later, I would return for a closer scrutiny. When circumstances required.

Shut the door. Very securely. So that, when M. returned home, she would have no reason to think that anyone had violated her precious privacy.

By this time busybodies from the college begun to call my father, informing him that Marguerite hadn't come to the college that day, she'd missed appointments "which wasn't like Marguerite" and so they were wondering if she was home, and if she was all right; and Father sent Lena to check M.'s room, which was (of course, as I knew) empty, and Father went himself to check the garage where M.'s pale yellow Volvo was parked beside his stately black Lincoln sedan: still, nothing out of the ordinary since M. rarely drove to the college.

But where, at this time of day, could M. *be*? Without her car, had to be on foot, so it was reasoned.

In fact M. often went for long walks/hikes by herself even in inhospitable weather. In hilly countryside beyond Drumlin Road, along wild, uncultivated stretches of Cayuga Lake where the shore was open, not fenced off by private landowners.

Preferring to walk alone. Though sometimes, who knows why, (wrongly) perceiving that I was looking lonely or wistful she'd invite me to join her.

31

Awkward and annoying, how M. would stride ahead on the trail as if (innocently) forgetting me then stop abruptly, and wait for me to catch up with her panting and perspiring.

The very image of patience. Not rolling her eyes, oh never.

Wondering then why I usually declined to join her. As if she had no idea.

"Georgene?"—there was Father peering nearsightedly at me over his bifocals having encountered me on the stairway landing where I happened to be standing staring out a window at curious-shaped clouds blown overhead like a ragged flotilla of sailing ships, my mind utterly blank as a hosed-down wall.

At this time of day Father was usually absorbed in work. In his office in downtown Aurora or in his home office at the rear of the house conferring by phone with investment advisors in New York City, directing stocks to be purchased, stocks to be sold, with the vehemence of a warrior doling out rewards and punishments. From childhood we'd known not to interrupt Father at such times—(as if we'd had any reason to interrupt him!)—but here suddenly was Father looking disoriented like one who has lost his way, agitated, distracted (fortunately not noticing how I guiltily hid what was in my hand, some trivial item from M.'s room, a small piece of inexpensive jewelry M. would never miss, unless it was a

[used] tube of Midnight Rose lipstick, essentially of no use to me who would no more smear makeup on my face than I would smear putty on my face with a trowel and rub clown spots of rouge on my "chubby" cheeks) asking if I remembered having seen Marguerite at any time that day and through a beating of blood in my ears I didn't hear this question, and Father repeated the question, and a scream surprised us both erupting from my lips:

"No! I *have not* seen Marguerite, not since this morning, why is everyone always asking me about *her*!"

◆

Soon then, relatives began to call. In Aurora-on-Cayuga, news spreads rapidly.

Where is Marguerite? Have you heard from Marguerite? Have you seen anyone who has seen Marguerite?

Scarcely was M. missing eight hours, already word was out that *something must have happened to M., this is not like M.*

Yes, it was ridiculous! Only I seemed to know.

Father insisted upon answering these calls. Not even allowing Lena to pick up the phone.

Fatherly voice of "command." Loud voice of a man who is accustomed to being listened to. Loud voice of one who is hard of hearing. Though relatives were calling to

33

ask about M., Father fired back questions at them like an irascible Ping-Pong player firing back shots.

Any news of his daughter? Had Marguerite called any of them? Had Marguerite gone out of town, without telling them? Marguerite had friends over in Ithaca—was Marguerite (maybe) in Ithaca?

(But if so, why was Marguerite's car in the garage?)

(This would be cited as proof that M. hadn't gone away of her own accord—the Volvo in the garage! As if that proved anything.)

Another time, the impetuous *senior artist-in-residence* at the college called, daring to ask Father if there was some "private phone line" with which to contact Marguerite, about a "strictly personal matter"; and Father said coldly, "Sir, whoever you are, I don't care if you are a 'colleague' of my daughter's or not, the name 'Elke' is not known to me, and that information is none of your business. Goodbye!"

(At the time we did not think it odd, that "Elke" was making such a pest of himself, as if there were, indeed, some particular connection between him and M., of which we hadn't known.)

Too restless to remain indoors Father insisted upon driving through the village in the stately black Lincoln slow along Main Street past darkened storefronts (several of these properties owned by Father, in fact), turning onto Lakeview Avenue passing the large, lighted homes of Fulmer relatives, aunts, uncles, cousins of whom some were a wee bit more tolerable to M. and to me than the others, but none of whom were close to M. to the degree that she might have simply stopped by to visit without informing us; as Father sniffed and peered at the first of these residences, as if about to turn into the driveway, I said, sharply: "Father, *no*. Don't give them the satisfaction."

And Father sighed: yes, of course. The last thing Marguerite would wish, her envious cousins chattering about her *going missing*.

Continuing slow along Church Street past the "historic" darkened cemetery out of which weatherworn tombstones glowed with the eerie luminosity of radioactive teeth taunting our foolish and futile quest.

Sharp uphill onto the Aurora College campus, stark red-brick buildings lonely as frigates riding the crest of an inland sea. Bell tower, chapel. Dull tolling of the hour 9 P.M. and the white clockface illuminated like the very face of idiocy devoid of human expression.

She hadn't wanted to return to Aurora-on-Cayuga. Her return was "temporary."

Nervy and condescending that she'd come home from New York City for *me*. Maybe she'd been jealous of *me*.

35

It was after Mother's death. Which (I guess: I don't remember clearly) I'd taken pretty hard.

Though I had not loved Mother—not *much.*

But then I don't love anyone—*much.*

M. had accepted the position at the college with the understanding that her (modest) salary would be channeled into a fund for scholarships. But in utmost secrecy, for M. did not wish to be known as any sort of "philanthropist," she did not want her artist-colleagues (most of whom were older than she) to feel uneasy in her presence.

Of course they were inferior to Marguerite Fulmer. And made to know it.

Any one of them might have wished her harm.

Our family had long been prominent in Aurora and vicinity. Father's father and grandfather had been trustees of the women's college, as Father was now; they were a family of bankers, investors, real estate developers, philanthropists. To M.'s embarrassment, one of the older and more dignified red-brick buildings on the campus was Fulmer Hall.

Mother, too, had been "from a good family"—of course! Never doubt.

A family in which, it would be revealed, women had a predilection for a certain sort of cancer. And a predilection for dying of this cancer.

The specificity of which, I think, I do not care to disclose.

I wondered if Father was thinking such somber thoughts. If Father dared think of the loss of Mother, which had torn our solid-seeming household in two.

Frowning and sternly glaring driving slow along curving campus roads pausing to stare into the darkness between buildings and into shadows that, when exposed by headlights, were flat and banal as the interior of a cardboard box.

Beside Father in the passenger's seat of the Lincoln sedan I sat with my fists between my knees gripped tight to keep from shifting and twitching for I am restless at such times not daring to speak aloud what clamors to be said—*Do you really think Marguerite is skulking in the shadows here, Father? Do you really think you will find her here?*

If the Princess does not want to be found, the Princess will not be found.

Sighting a lone female figure on a walkway outside the college library Father braked the car to a stop and fumbled to lower the window—"Marguerite? Is that you?"

His voice cracked. I'd have wanted to laugh but realized suddenly that Father was truly upset.

Fortunately the girl didn't hear. Hurrying past us clutching her books to her chest without a backward glance.

8

That Interminable Day. By 10 P.M. that night a light rain had begun to fall. I stood by an upstairs window gazing out into the night thinking *She will get wet now, and cold! Now, Princess will come meekly home like a dog with its tail between its legs.*

Still, by 11 P.M. M. had not returned home, nor had she called to explain where she was; nor had anyone called on her behalf.

Was I beginning to be frightened, yes I was beginning to be frightened because a great wave of dirty water was rushing at us though our house is on a hill above the town and *I do not like upset.*

I do not like upset (unless it is an upset that I have caused myself). I do not like a violation of the household

38

routine. I believe that there is nothing so upsetting as a violation of the household routine. I am on duty behind the counter at the Mill Street Post Office for eight hours five days a week and when I am not at my post at the post office I am safe and quiet in my room in my father's house where I do not like a violation of our domestic routine like supper postponed for hours, kept in a warm oven by Lena and tasteless as last week's leftovers and above all I do not like the damned telephone jingling and jangling and no calls ever for *me*, always for *her*.

It was clear, no one would sleep that night in our house. Nine hours is required for me to sleep if I am to be clear-minded and suffused with energy in the morning to face eight hours upright and "customer-friendly" at the post office but there was not the slightest care for me, not that this was surprising of course it was not.

At last Father called 911. Others had encouraged him, excitable relatives who lived a block away on Lakeview Avenue, and (of course) Lena, wringing her hands with worry over my sister, so Father made the call, hesitant in his speech, faltering, uncertain, revealed as a man on the brink of being *old*.

Yes, an emergency!—"I have reason to think that my daughter Marguerite is in grave danger."

Telling the (two, uniformed) police officers who arrived at our house that something must have happened to M., she'd been missing all day, hadn't appeared at the college as she was expected, *it was not like his daughter to behave so irresponsibly.* Should have known that something was wrong, he hadn't seen M. at breakfast that morning. (As if the three of us routinely had breakfast together! Sometimes we did, but only by chance. Since Mother's illness and death our mealtimes were not formal affairs. Often, Marguerite skipped breakfast altogether. Or, if she had breakfast, it was at the college, in the cafeteria. My breakfast is my own business. I might have Cheerios with banana and milk at the house, and a second, larger breakfast at the diner across from the post office—scrambled eggs and bacon, rye toast and grape jelly. Father might have just black coffee and oatmeal prepared by Lena, as late as 11 A.M. on one of his dark-mood mornings.)

Not like my daughter to behave irresponsibly was several times repeated as if this statement were profound in itself and would impress the police officers as it seemed to impress Father.

Of the policemen one of them was distinctly younger than the other. To my disgust I recognized the callow porcine face of a boy who'd gone to my high school now grown beefy, swarthy-jawed blinking and squinting at the

40

high-ceilinged interior of the English Tudor on Cayuga Avenue where otherwise he'd never have been invited to set foot like any of his ilk.

And staring at me startled. As if he did not, yet did, recognize me but dared not acknowledge me as I scorned to acknowledge him.

For "Georgene Fulmer" has changed much since high school days, I think.

Both my face, and my body. Where once I was weak now I am sturdy as a turnip.

Where once I was vulnerable to fools and bullies now I am impervious as a mollusk that, when you peer at it, all you see is a fine-ridged shell and not a bit of pink exposed flesh.

The elder policeman spoke with ponderous slowness like a hippopotamus summoning speech. *Maybe your daughter is away for the night Mr. Fulmer but will return in the morning, we see that lots of times. Doesn't mean that she's a runaway.*

Runaway! So ridiculous, I burst into derisive laughter.

Both policemen stared at me astonished. Father stared at me, disapproving.

The elder policeman asked me what was so funny and I told the fool point-blank that my sister Marguerite wasn't a teenager, she was thirty years old, artist-in-residence at

Aurora College and an accomplished sculptor, hardly a *runaway.*

Father laid a hand on my arm to calm me, for I was laughing hard, and then I was coughing, and both policemen were staring at me at too close quarters.

Such fools!—I gave up on them, left the room heavy-footed on the stairs and slammed the door to my own room.

Thinking—*Now they will search M.'s room. Now they will search the entire house.*

Attic to basement. Three floors. In the "new" basement, which is finished, and in the "old" basement where no one ever treads that has an earthen floor smelling of rancid damp and rot.

But no: they did not search M.'s room that night, still less the entire house.

◆

This day! This day! This damned day.

So very long, at one end you could not see the beginning in a haze like mist rising on the lake and drifting inland. Someone with good intentions had switched on all the lights in the house and the house was ablaze like a Hallowe'en pumpkin announcing to all of Aurora

42

that something had happened at 188 Cayuga Avenue: but what?

And all of this M.'s fault, calling such attention to herself, always the center of attention, *I hated her and would never forgive her.*

9

The Search. Rarely in the history of Aurora and its rural surroundings had adults been reported missing; more commonly, teenaged girls who vanished from their homes were labeled *runaways.* Rarely had there been serious crimes here: a single homicide in eighty years, which would have been labeled *domestic violence* in contemporary times.

No kidnappings, no abductions—if rapes, sexual assaults, beatings, these were not reported to police, consequently were not on the record.

The most common crime in Aurora and surroundings was (teenaged) vandalism: graffiti, mailbox bashing, dumped trash, and fires in fields on Hallowe'en.

And so now in April 1991, confronted with the myste-
rious disappearance of a local *heiress*, the four-man Aurora
Police Department required assistance from the Cayuga
County Sheriff's Department.

Twenty-four hours is generally considered by law
enforcement agencies too short a period of time for an
adult to be declared officially missing but circumstances,
and Father's insistence, as well as Father's social position
in Aurora, suggested that Marguerite Fulmer's disappearance had to be taken seriously. Local media was alerted,
TV and radio bulletins were broadcast striving for a tone
somewhere between excitable-alarmed and dignified-
restrained. Astonishing to turn on the TV and see M.'s face
gazing out at us above the caption *Aurora woman reported
missing overnight by family.*

On the morning of April 12 search parties were organized to look for my sister, now acknowledged to have
been missing for twenty-four hours. Law enforcement
officers, volunteer firemen of Cayuga County, high
school students released from classes for the occasion,
strapping young female athletes from Aurora College,
citizen-volunteers from the community. Later in the
day, Cornell University students who'd heard the news
bulletins about the *missing woman* for whose sake a
$50,000 reward was being offered by her family made the

hour's journey around the lake from Ithaca in a caravan of vehicles.

Father had wished to offer $100,000 but had been discouraged by detectives who worried that so high a sum would attract too much attention which would be *counterproductive.*

Already police were receiving calls of "sightings"— "suspicious persons"—in places they should not have been. TV and radio stations were beginning to receive calls, which would escalate alarmingly in subsequent days.

Each lead, we were assured by police, would be followed. One of myriad lies in a succession of lies stretching through the decade to come, and beyond.

It was determined, by Lena and me, that no suitcases of M.'s seemed to be missing from her closet. No clothes seemed to be visibly missing. (Though indeed Lena would have agreed with anything I said, in my definite way; Lena was not one to contradict.) M.'s wristwatch was a silver Longines bracelet-watch with a smoky-dark face and small silver numerals which only the wearer could see; M. was rarely without this striking piece of jewelry, another of her New York purchases, and had surely worn it that morning. When M. worked in her studio she didn't wear rings; yet, I thought I remembered seeing, on M.'s hand, that morning, the amethyst ring that had once belonged to our grandmother. . . . (Which ring I would later discover in my bottom bureau drawer, no idea how it had gotten there!)

Lena and I were in agreement, M. had surely taken with her the hemp-woven shoulder bag she used routinely, not one of her more expensive leather bags, left behind in her room; this bag containing her (Prada) wallet and other personal items.

By midday of April 12 there had been no credit card activity on her account. No withdrawal from her savings account at the Bank of Cayuga.

There was never to be any "activity" on M.'s accounts. Whether this was good news, not-so-good news, or neutral, was a matter of speculation.

Yes! I intended to join one of the search parties: the girl-athletes at Aurora College.

Except I'd slept very poorly that night. My legs were strangely leaden, a dull pain throbbed behind my eyes. Barely could I make my way downstairs. I had no appetite for breakfast, to Lena's distress; for Lena knew how light-headed I might be, if I went without breakfast. She had to steady me as I tried to jam my feet (in woolen socks) into (rubber) boots, panting and cursing. But by the time I hiked over to Aurora College the search party had set off without me, there was no reasonable hope of my catching up.

47

Could have wept with frustration, disappointment! Girl-athletes hiking through fields, united in the common cause of looking for my sister, and I was not among them. . . .

Other search parties did not interest me. Fulmer relatives—cousins, nieces, nephews, tramping through fields with a hope of seeing themselves on TV news that night—particularly did not interest me.

Seemed like forever passing out flyers and posters in town. Of course I was anxious but the main feeling was boredom. People gaping at me, asking damn-fool questions. *Are you her sister? When did you see her last? How did she seem?*

Public library bulletin boards, community center, post office. Had to laugh, seeing *Marguerite Fulmer* side by side with *FBI Most Wanted*.

Weird to see M.'s face everywhere in Aurora and below it the headline MISSING: MARGUERITE FULMER.

It seemed cruel, M. was smiling in the photograph. Looking happy, confident. No idea what was coming for her.

A very good reason never to smile when your picture is being taken, yes?

The shiny little arrow-shaped scar in M.'s left cheek just below her left eye did not show in the photograph. Though I stared and stared, and brought the poster into the light where I could see better, I could not detect it.

10

Heiress. The first (local) media headlines were *Missing Aurora Woman,* by the next day altered to *Missing Aurora Heiress* to be promulgated through New York State, syndicated by the Associated Press, and by April 17, 1991, find its way into the magisterial *New York Times.*

And once M. was identified as a *missing heiress,* she would never again be identified as merely a *missing woman;* nor would much be said about her career as a *sculptor* except that, true to the tradition of superficial journalism, M. might be identified as a *former Guggenheim fellow.*

Indeed, very little would be made of M.'s art, which was "abstract"—"non-representational"—think elegant Kandinsky, Brancusi, Moore and not the more popular feminists Marisol, Bourgeois, Kahlo; no figurative work, no outrageous images which the media could present to suggest that there might be some connection between the *sculptress* and her fate as *missing*.

Yes, it was a shame! An insult.

Reducing a woman artist to *heiress*. When nothing in M.'s life had interested her less than her identity as an *heiress*. And nothing in her life interested her more than her identity as an *artist*.

◆

But this reminds me, a jab in the ribs: *You are an heiress too.*

Father's estate will fall to *me*, one day. And this house, and this property. Unless Marguerite returns, in which case we will share equally.

11

The Artist M. Clues in M.'s sculptures?—naturally, people wondered.

As if a clue to what had happened to M., where M. *was,* might be found in her art: a half-dozen unfinished sculptures in her studio at the college.

As a professional artist M. exhibited her work under the coyly androgynous name "M. Fulmer." M.'s sculptures were what's called "abstract." Vivid-white, gray-white, bluish-white, sulphurous-white. Most were made of some sort of natural stone or rock, chiseled, chipped, sanded, polished by hand, requiring hundreds of hours of the sculptor's labor; yet, to my eye, baffling, annoying.

I was not an admirer of M.'s art. I was not an admirer of M. as an *artiste*. Not because M.'s art took her away from Aurora, connecting her to a world elsewhere, centered (for instance) in New York City, flattering her with awards, fellowships (the "prestigious" Guggenheim, surely not merited at M.'s callow young age)—but because M.'s art was prissy, self-conscious, impersonal. *Too perfect.*

Ovoid, rectangular, geometrical in shape, only obliquely suggesting human figures and human features—you could walk around these sculptures, resting on pedestals, or on the floor, of a height of about five feet, just stare and stare and never make sense of them, like trying to see a human face in the clouds, or in a patch of mud. You think—*But why am I looking at this, what am I supposed to see?*—and there is never any answer.

Beautiful but bland. "Striking" but forgettable. Enigmatic but pretentious.

Maddening! Makes you want to smash the so-called *work of art.*

(Not that I ever did. Though I had the opportunity. The most I'd done was make some scratches with my Swiss army knife on one of M.'s sculptures exhibited at Aurora College, on its underside, where, I think, M. never saw; or, if she saw, never said a word of which I knew. And once or twice when I was much younger, when M. was working at home, I might have deliberately smudged a pristine-white oval resembling a head, with my dirty hands.)

Photographs of the sculptures at the art school were taken for police files, to be examined, we were told gravely, by "forensic arts specialists." (What a joke!) Some of these photographs made their way into print without our permission. Onto TV.

M. would have been mortified. Never would she have allowed her work to be photographed before it was finished. (But how could you tell if M.'s work *was* finished?— much of it looked the same to me.)

Yet, earlier work of M.'s (including several pieces that had won awards) didn't look very different from the newer work. M. liked to describe herself as "formalist"— "classicist"—"minimalist." The sort of sculptures that inspire the ignorant to say with a smirk, "I could do that!"

(Well, isn't it true? I've often thought, looking at my sister's much-lauded work, that indeed *I* could have done it—if I'd thought of it.)

(I've had that exact thought about the so-called Abstract Expressionists, whom M. professed to admire. Pollock, Rothko, de Kooning—*I* could have painted their slovenly

53

paintings if I'd thought of it; you wouldn't need a talent for *drawing* like Leonardo da Vinci or what's-his-name up in Maine—Andrew Wyeth.)

Ovoid 90 would come to be M.'s best-known sculpture, frequently reproduced after her death. Smooth grayish-white stone like a gigantic egg, or a weirdly shaped grave marker with quirky little indentations like hieroglyphics and miniature protrusions like aborted tendrils, of a size and weight to make it unwieldy—four feet high, five feet in circumference, but irregular, just perceptibly wider at the bottom than at the top. And far too heavy to be easily moved about.

It was claimed that the sculptor had worked no less than one thousand hours on *Ovoid 90*. An unimpressed observer (like G.) might ask skeptically *Why?*

Even so, M. hadn't quite finished with *Ovoid 90* at the time she'd disappeared.

(Not that anyone could tell that the spherical thing wasn't finished! But I didn't say that.)

Indeed, Father and I have donated *Ovoid 90* to Aurora College, where, following a ceremony involving the college president, the dean of the arts school, and Father himself white-haired and gravely handsome as a heroic statue, if stooped by sorrow, the sculpture is to preside forever on a scenic hill beyond the library.

Insipid Ovoid, is what I call it. (Secretly!)

(For when we were growing up nosy busybodies in the family speculated *Poor Georgene!—she must be so envious of Marguerite* but I refuted them utterly by refusing to be envious of anyone, ever.)

What are called "works-in-progress"—as well as worksheets, sketches, notebooks, etc. in M.'s studio—were returned to Father and me at the end of the 1991 spring semester at Aurora College; by which time police investigators, including so-called forensic experts, had finished examining them, having made "nothing conclusive" of them as they'd made "nothing conclusive" of anything.

Especially, the fools were unaware of what was missing. For how'd they know what was missing?

For instance: if there'd been an artist's journal among M.'s things, something like a personal journal or diary, naturally I'd removed that as soon as I laid eyes on it, on the afternoon of April 12, 1991: not for vulgar strangers, the perusal of my sister's secrets.

12

Ms. Fulmer can you think of anyone who might wish to harm your sister? Any enemies of your sister? Any men involved with your sister?

No, no and *no.*

Vehemently, defiantly—*no.*

13

(Obviously the sister isn't trying to direct the investigation away from herself. She didn't give us a single name.)

14

Jealousy. No revenge without jealousy, the struck match.

Most mysterious of emotions. Most *shameful* of emotions.

If one thing is clear in my nature it is that I am immune to such adolescent emotions as *jealousy, envy, spite, vindictiveness.* I scorn weakness in all, but most in my*self.*

Of the men who'd loved M. each had hoped to "possess" her.

(I have put quotation marks around this word to indicate that yes, I think it's a silly word. I think it's a silly wish. But I understand that the wish to "possess" is a wish of many men confounded by a woman who eludes them.)

Not that M. told me much about her private life. *Her* life was precious to her—not to be shared with a callow younger sister.

But I knew of "W."—who'd actually come to the house seeking her. And there were others—"D."—"Y."—"T."— whom I'd never met but knew of, circuitously. And there would turn out to be others.

Each of them men with whom M. had been (possibly) involved. (Possibly) sexually involved. In Ithaca, in New York City, even in Aurora over a period of years.

I would not name these names. *I* would not lower myself by repeating crude and prurient gossip.

In fact, with one exception I did not know the men's names—not their full names. Others in the family, our cousins, scattered friends and former high school class-mates of M.'s not above repeating gossip under the guise of aiding the police in their investigation would name the names of "men in M.'s life" who would then be duly interviewed as *persons of interest.*

Malicious delight in the *naming of names.* How easy it is to complicate, perhaps even to ruin another's life, by "naming" him in an investigation of a young woman's disappearance.

Revenge on M. for having excited masculine interest, desire; and revenge on the *persons of interest* for having had such desire.

In time, the police investigation would widen to add many more names. Not in depth but in breadth the (futile) investigation sprawled. For a police investigation into an "unsolved" crime will have no boundaries and, in theory, no end.

Like those paths through the woods hopelessly criss-crossed with the footprints of strangers and even the hoofprints of deer, a tangle of "clues" leading nowhere.

A police investigation "still open"—"pending"—means no mercy for anyone involved.

No end to a police investigation means sorrow yielding to anger, and anger yielding to sorrow.

How does a *person of interest* become a *suspect*?

Here is where police failed. There would not be a singular *suspect*.

A collective story emerged as if out of the mist: he'd picked her up on Drumlin Road. Whoever it was, who'd carried M. away.

Forced her into his vehicle—possibly into the trunk. Tied her, gagged her, hauled her away still alive, to an uncertain fate.

Unless: on Drumlin Road she'd stepped into the vehicle as planned. Breathless and yearning and having brought with her virtually no personal possessions and (probably) less than one hundred dollars in cash in her wallet, judging by the most recent withdrawal from M.'s savings account at the Bank of Cayuga, which had been less than five hundred dollars and had not in fact been recent.

In which case, who was driving the vehicle? And where was the vehicle driven, after Drumlin Road?

◆

Jealousy! I was not *jealous* of the (alleged) men in M.'s life because I was not jealous of M. A younger sister can't plausibly be jealous of an older accomplished beautiful sister, she can only be in awe of such a sister, grateful for attention from the Princess, fleeting smiles, words of approval now and then tossed like coins.

Were you and your sister close? Did you become closer after your mother's death?

Did your sister confide in you?

No, no, and *never.*

15

Abduction. Eventually it would come to seem most likely that *abduction* was the (probable) explanation for M.'s disappearance.

That is, a consensus of police, journalists, local authorities, family, relatives, residents of Aurora, and, in time, assorted amateur aficionados of (unsolved) mysteries, some of them very ignorant, annoying, and offensive persons, indeed.

In the crazed days immediately following M.'s disappearance, when "sightings" of my sister were being reported throughout the Finger Lakes region in New York State and beyond, and Aurora police officers were stationed round-the-clock at 188 Cayuga Avenue to protect our beleaguered house from unwanted visitors (unauthorized journalists, TV crews, volunteers, and vigilantes of all kinds) *kidnapping* had (also) been a possibility.

Of course, considering the social prominence of the *missing woman/heiress*, kidnapping would have been plausible.

Through Cayuga County the name "Fulmer" evoked wealth, stature, privilege.

(Exaggerated, of course! As everything is exaggerated in small-town America where to be "rich" is just to have a little more money than most other residents.)

Detectives had advised Father to alert them immediately if kidnappers contacted him, not to attempt to negotiate with anyone, and certainly not to pay anyone any ransom, to which Father agreed, for Father was, as he liked to boast, "no fool"; yet, I am sure that if kidnappers had called him, if M. had spoken with Father on the phone pleading for her life, in a heartbeat Father would have capitulated.

But no kidnappers contacted Father. No ransom was (ever) demanded.

The phone rang maddeningly often in those days, for detectives told us that we should keep the phone on the hook and answer it; yet, it was never *the* call.

Each ring of the phone, a leap of the heart; each disappointing call, a sinking of the heart.

And so, barring kidnapping, increasingly it looked as if M. had been *abducted*.

In this case there would never be a call but (cruelly) a proliferation of days of awaiting the call never to come for, if *abduction*, as police allowed us to know, it was likely that M. was no longer living and it was likely that her whereabouts would never be known; most abductions of young women, girls, children end in death, sexual mutilation, hideous death; many/most bodies of such victims are never found though there is the (rare) possibility that the murderer will one day confess to a prison cellmate (for instance) or in the final days of his life suddenly plead for mercy from God.

Contemplating these possibilities Father drank Scotch whisky solemnly shaking his head.

"Not at all. No. We will see Marguerite again. *I have a feeling.*"

16

Legal Rules & Procedures Defining Missing Persons (New York State)

23.0 A missing person is one who is reported "missing" from a residence and is:

    a. Under 18, or

    b. 18 or over, and:

        1. mentally or physically affected to the extent that hospitalization may be required, or

        2. a possible victim of amnesia, drowning, or similar mishap, or

3. has indicated an intention of commit-
   ting suicide, or
4. absent without any evident reason
   under circumstances indicating invol-
   untary disappearance.

23.1 The term "missing person" shall not include a person:

    a. for whom warrants have been issued

    b. wanted for commission of a crime

    c. 18 or older, who voluntarily leaves home for
domestic, financial, or similar reasons

    d. fitting the designation "voluntary absentee"

17

The Wallet. Though soaked with rain, battered and muddy, the black leather wallet wasn't old or worn. No cash remained in it, no credit cards or identification, the wallet flat, sadly inconsequential except for the designer's shiny metal label—*Prada.*

Found by the side of a country road (eight miles east of Aurora, a quarter mile from the entrance to the New York Thruway), nearly a month after M. had disappeared, by a teenaged bicyclist who'd seen it lying "in plain view" like trash tossed from a passing vehicle.

Weeks had passed by this time, there had been no activity on M.'s credit cards. Father had arranged to shut down all her accounts.

Was the battered wallet M.'s? It was true, M. had had a *Prada* wallet, purchased in New York City years ago. As M. had owned other designer items, including the silky white Dior dress, purchased in New York City at some time during those (three) years she'd lived there.

Note that much is hypothetical here. Though G. may know *exactly what has happened to M.*, G. is taking care to present "clues" as they appear in sequence.

Fulmer relatives were convinced that the battered wallet was M.'s. Father had to suppose, yes it was. Even those who'd never actually seen M.'s wallet or had the slightest idea of what a wallet of M.'s might look like were convinced—*This had to be her wallet!*

And if it was M.'s wallet this was proof that M. had been forcibly abducted from Aurora and had not left Aurora of her own volition. Classified as a "missing person, suspected foul play" and not a "voluntary absentee."

Except G., the younger sister, was not one of these (gullible) persons.

Ever skeptical, resistant to "believing" what others believed so unquestioningly.

Convinced at a glance that the wallet found so conveniently by the roadside was not my sister's wallet.

But—isn't this "evidence"? A "clue"?

Too obviously "evidence"—a "clue." Too obvious to be true.

In exasperation they asked me why I would say such a thing, obviously the wallet was M.'s, for God's sake how many *Prada* wallets would there be in Cayuga County!— especially wallets discarded by the roadside shortly after M. had gone missing.

Because I have my reasons. Because I am not such a fool, to take at face value a wallet that has been, or might have been, *planted*.

Tossed by the roadside, in a visible place. *Not* tossed, inconveniently, in tall weeds, or in a ditch, or into Cayuga Lake.

Tossed by the roadside by M. herself, like trash. Possibly.

As she was tossing away her Aurora life like trash with no more concern for those (of us) who loved her as for those (of us) who disapproved of her.

"Georgene, you're being ridiculous. Don't you *want* the police to find Marguerite?"

Our cousin Denise, M.'s age, once close to M. in high school, now absorbed in her smug wife/mother life, daring to jeer at *me*.

Staring at Denise's doughy made-up face, wanting badly to slap her.

Feeling my own face suffuse with blood, heat. Tears of fury in my eyes.

And then—with great dignity—*not* slapping Denise but turning away, walking away stiff-backed and indignant. Just walking away and leaving Denise staring after me.

Never. I will never. Never change my mind, I know what I know, that none of you will ever know.

◆

The battered Prada wallet "tentatively" identified as belonging to Marguerite Fulmer was kept in police files where it remains, I would assume, to this very day.

18

Chaos/clues. In our cold climate snow flurries are common in April. Snowflakes swirling in a chaos like clues in the wake of a mystery.

It is terrible to see, to realize, that the world is a *chaos of clues.*

Where there is no body, only a *missing body.* Where there is no assurance that the *missing body* is even alive.

Why was I the only person to recognize that the Prada wallet wasn't a clue but an *anti-clue*? That is, an item that purports to be a "clue" in the jigsaw puzzle of the mystery of M.'s disappearance but was, in fact, an "anti-clue"—a stratagem to confuse, not enlighten.

A trap to lead detectives into thinking that M. had been abducted, and her wallet tossed out the window of a vehicle headed for the Thruway. Probably.

Skeptical G. knows better: there would be no logic to tossing the wallet of an abducted woman out the window of a speeding car headed for the entrance of the Thruway. For *why?*

Obviously, staged. And *why staged?*—to mislead.

To make detectives think that the *missing person* is somewhere other than Aurora. To make detectives think that a crime has been committed and not a "voluntary" absence of the seemingly missing person.

Other clues the detectives may have missed. But G., perusing M.'s calendar since the start of 1991, noted.

Frequent pencil-notations on the calendar. Like anyone's calendar.

Amid a welter of notations of no interest, this for April 8 caught my eye: "MAM: 9 A.M."

And, for March 29: "MAM: 11 A.M."

Of course, I didn't mention this to anyone. My interactions with the detectives were as infrequent as I could make them without arousing suspicion.

◆

Another *anti-clue*. M.'s astrological chart.

Born on March 23, 1961, M. was what's called an "Aries."

(Born on August 18, 1967, G. is what's called a "Leo.")

Though I never graduated from college I am too much of a skeptic to subscribe to astrology—of course. Silly as "God" is, He makes more sense than "the stars."

The human brain, swamped with a chaos of clues, strains to comprehend what is incomprehensible. Even Einstein cried out in defiance: "God does not play dice with the universe!"

But probably yes, God *does* play dice with the universe.

If you fuss and fret enough, and are willing to expend as much time on your "birth chart" as you might expend learning something useful like high school calculus, you might draw a conclusion or two or three from the insipid fact that M. was born on March 23, and/or that I was born on August 18, and that Aries and Leo interact in certain fixed ways that assure *strife, rivalry, struggle, conquest.* You might learn that Aries personalities are "creative"— "imaginative"—"thoughtful"—"kind"—"disciplined, well-organized" but also "insensitive of others"— "impatient"—"stubborn." You might learn that Leo person-alities are "loyal"—"truth-loving"—"independent-minded"

73

but also "demanding of deep devotion" and "prone to jealousy and possessiveness."

Ridiculous! Totally baseless.

Genetics, prenatal care, and environmental circumstances, not the stars, determine the essential nature of a human personality. Astrology is a long-discredited worthless pseudoscience.

Yet, to our dismay and disgust, an Aurora resident named Mildred Pfeiffer who knew nothing of the Fulmer family, and certainly nothing of Marguerite, who dared to call herself an *astrological psychic voyager*, took it upon herself to draw an extensive astrological chart based on my sister's birthdate and the date of her disappearance, boasting that her calculations could "solve the mystery."

First, this shameless publicity-seeker tried to meet with Father, and was soundly rebuffed by our housekeeper; tried to meet with me, and was soundly rebuffed by *me*.

Next, most brazenly, Mildred Pfeiffer went to Aurora police headquarters to demand to speak with the detectives investigating the case, and was rebuffed a third time.

But next, undeterred, Pfieffer dared to knock on the door of Fulmer relatives living on Lakeview Avenue who were naive enough, or malicious enough, to invite the self-styled *astrological psychic voyager* inside, to listen to her mad prattling.

Next morning cousin Denise called me to report.

But quickly I interrupted: "Just—stop, Denise. I am going to hang up."

"Georgene, wait! The woman had some interesting insights—"

"She *did not,* she *could not* have had 'interesting insights.' Astrology is sheer superstition. 'Psychics' are charlatans. I am going to hang up now."

My voice was quaking. It came to me in waves, how I'd *hated* this girl-cousin of mine, M.'s closest friend among the girl-cousins when they were in high school.

Denise protested: "No, Georgene, wait! This person says that she can 'see'—"

"She *cannot see.* She has concocted nonsense for fools to believe, that will end up in the newspaper unless we stop her *now.*"

Adding, furiously: "Marguerite did not believe in 'signs'—Father and I do not believe in 'signs.' This is insulting."

"Georgene, please don't shout! I can hear you clearly. What Mildred Pfeiffer is saying is that according to her calculations Marguerite is still here—in Aurora. She can 'see'—she says—through Marguerite's eyes—(she's something of a psychic too)—but her vision is 'dark, clouded.' She has tried to contact Marguerite but says that Marguerite is 'mute'—doesn't reply . . ."

"Denise, this is utterly ridiculous. You must be trying to upset me. Please do not dare to contact my father—*do not*. This woman is a shameless huckster, she will be wanting money from us. She wants that fifty thousand dollars from Father! If you're in contact with her tell her that she *cannot dare to intrude in Marguerite's life*. If she persists, tell her that I will kill her."

"Georgene, what are you saying? You will *kill*—?"

"I will sue her. I said—*sue*. And I am hanging up now, this ridiculous conversation has gone on long enough."

Slamming down the receiver so hard it fell clattering to the floor.

19

"*Psychic Voyager.*" It was my mistake, I see now. Not taking Mildred Pfeiffer seriously.

Assuming that, since we were living, not in the twelfth century, but in the twentieth century, no one could really *take seriously* the nonsense-babble of astrology; let alone the nonsense-babble of a "psychic."

And so, after I continued to hear troubling reports from relatives, and after Pfeiffer tried to contact Father, and me, another time, I replied in this way:

> May 8, 1991
> Dear Mildred Pfeiffer,
>   Thank you for your concern on the behalf of my sister Marguerite.

I am afraid that, as devout Christians, of the Anglican persuasion, my father and I are obliged, in willing conformity to the principles of our Church, to profess no faith in astrology.

This is not to criticize or denigrate your calling. This is only to explain our wish not to be involved with your "findings"; and to make a heartfelt plea, that you cease and desist involving my sister, who cannot speak for herself in this matter, imagining that you have "access" to Marguerite's spirit and could in any way speak for her.

Thanking you beforehand, you miserable fraud—

Georgene Fulmer

◆

(No: I did not actually say "miserable fraud." Just a joke!)

But the rest of the letter was mailed to Ms. Pfeiffer as is. Not surprisingly, I did not receive a reply.

20

The End of the Beginning. One of the *persons of interest* whose name was passed on to detectives was "W."—"Walter Lang."

Of the men whose bad luck it was to have been involved with M., Walter Lang was the only one I'd ever set eyes on, several years before April 11, 1991.

No: I did not give police Walter Lang's name. Though I bitterly resented the way Walter Lang had treated me I did not wish the hapless man ill; I did not wish him tangled in the slovenly police investigation.

Poor Walter had showed up (uninvited) one day at our house. Unshaven, unkempt, anxious and apologetic hoping to speak with Milton Fulmer whom he'd never met, about why so abruptly and mysteriously M. had stopped seeing him, and had departed for New York City with only a telephone message goodbye—as if Father would have any idea what M.'s motives were! Or any patience, discussing them.

But Father took pity on this Walter, unexpectedly. Invited the distraught young man into the house instead of sending him away as I'd have predicted. Listened to him sympathetically for quite a while. Embarrassed that his daughter seemed to have behaved so capriciously with a man who (it appeared) loved her very much.

This Walter, I didn't know. Not personally. Later it would turn out that he was a research biologist at Cornell, whom M. had met through mutual acquaintances; a "highly promising" post-doc from Harvard who'd been seeing M. for several months, but whom M. had never gotten around to introducing to her family.

Daring to eavesdrop outside Father's office. My heart beating hard.

Did I feel sorry for "Walter"?—I did not.

Would-be lover of my sister. Would-be husband. Weak-willed, to fall under the (trite, predictable) sex-spell of the Princess.

Through the closed door of Father's office, Walter's despairing young voice was sounding earnestly, pleadingly.

Asking Father if he knew, if he had any idea, why M. had stopped seeing him? Wouldn't answer his calls?

Why she'd never spoken of Walter to us? Why she'd never invited him to the house?

How shocked Father must have been to meet Walter Lang—about whom he knew nothing.

(But that was always the way with M.: secretive. Not confiding.)

For forty minutes the men spoke together, in grave tones, in Father's office. This was amazing to me for two reasons: the first, that Father seemed to be tolerating the aggrieved young man, instead of ridiculing him; the second, that Father should speak to a stranger for so long on any subject when, I was sure, he'd never spoken to me for so many minutes at a time about anything; scarcely, indeed, for more than four minutes at a time.

For what is there to *say*, when so much must be left *unsaid*?

And how bitter it was to me, that two men should, for forty minutes, or four, so gravely discuss the whims of my sister's heart; sickening to me, the fury-knowledge that never, but never, will any men discuss *me*.

Wanting to laugh loudly and rudely so that this insipid Walter would hear me. So that both men would hear me.

Fool fool fool—what did you expect?

Until at last the conversation ended. The door to Father's office opened, Father saw the unhappy young man to the front door.

From the landing I observed them in the foyer below. It was not like Father, in my experience of him, to be so *kindly* with a fool, whether a "highly promising" research scientist or otherwise; it was not like Father to be so friendly toward a stranger with a sexual interest in his daughter.

Stammered words lifted to me on the landing above: "I hope I can see you again, Mr. Fulmer . . ."

And Father's terse reply: "Well. We will see, son."

Son! That odd, unexpected word, like a nudge in (my) ribs.

Father extended his hand for a brusque handshake. The visit was over.

On the front walk Walter Lang checked his bearings. Disoriented, hesitant like one who has forgotten where he is, or why.

Glancing back at the house, at the second-floor windows, with a look of such grief, such yearning, it was clear to any observer that the poor fool half expected M. to be watching him from one of the windows.

But no: no one was watching from the second-floor windows.

No one was going to wave to the rejected suitor from the second-floor windows.

Walter Lang's car, a battered-looking Ford, was parked at the curb at the end of our long pebbled driveway. And how fitting a vehicle for Walter, a bearish young man, slope-shouldered, with a large head, kindly if baffled eyes, not handsome, though not bad-looking. *Not Cary Grant, Clark Gable, but Fred MacMurray: stolid, easily baffled.*

And there suddenly I materialized at the curb. In the movie this might be a young Katharine Hepburn, not so "glamorous" as the original but no-nonsense, with cropped hair, slacks. Slightly panting from my run (from the side door of the house) along the driveway beneath tall oaks and yews to the strip of bright green grass at the curb.

Half my face a smile, half my face a sneer.

"Want my advice, Walter? Forget her."

Walter. The casual sound of his name, uttered by a stranger, had to be astonishing to him.

"First point: she doesn't deserve you."

I am the one who deserves you.

"Second point: she treats everyone like this. So don't feel singled-out."

I, too, have been spurned by her.

I, too, will have revenge.

A flush rose into Walter's face. Taken by surprise by this *chance encounter.*

For a delirious moment it looked to me—(as I stood smiling hard / not daring to breathe)—as if Walter would relax suddenly and laugh at my words, laugh at *me.* For it was a scene in a romantic comedy of the sort I (usually) scorned, in fact rarely watched on late-night TV.

We would begin speaking together, laughing together, like old friends, or at least old acquaintances knowing ourselves linked by a common wound.

"Are you Marguerite's sister?"

"I am numerous things, of which 'Marguerite's sister' is but one, and not the crucial one."

Truly, Walter appeared to be entranced by me! Just stared.

"Is it—Georgia? Georgene?"

"'G.' is sufficient."

"Well, hello—'G.'"

But it was a goodbye, not a hello. Clever repartee turns pathetic as used confetti when it fails to ignite.

What I'd hoped would be the beginning of a (thoroughly unexpected, delightful) romance turned out to be the end. The end of the *beginning,* to be precise.

For I did not—*do not*—resemble the young Katharine Hepburn. Any more than W. resembled Fred MacMurray.

Already opening the car door, ducking inside. Embarrassed to be confronted by me knowing that I knew what he'd have preferred no one knew, the humiliation, shock, shame of being rejected by a woman he believed he loved; and *no*, this was not a link between us that would define us or even survive these fleeting minutes as W. fumbled to start the car, avoiding my bright gleaming eyes while trying to be polite, nodding, smiling, eager to escape.

In this way breaking off the *chance encounter* that in a romantic comedy on late-night classic-film TV would have had a very different ending.

Driving away, descending Cayuga Avenue retracing his route. On his way back around the lake to Ithaca, not a backward glance.

And the younger sister G. left behind at the curb staring/glaring after the departing vehicle.

Telling herself she isn't surprised. No!

But still, she is furious. Heavy-jawed, impassive-faced as a crude Inuit carving in soapstone.

I am the one who deserves you. Fool! You will see.

21

The Cellar. Inside the (old, stone) cellar wall there had come jeering voices. Through the long winter and slow-dripping spring of 1991.

Slow-gathering for years. As pressure builds inside a volcano until the hot mad lava explodes. Nudge my head against the wall, to hurt. Ear against the wall, murmur of voices inside, derisive laughter.

Where I'd hidden from them hugging my fat knees against my chest.

Georg-ene! Georg-ene! Where're you hiding!

Not the "new" cellar with a tile floor, gleaming new furnace and hot water heater, exposed pipes, windows emitting a greeny-scummy light, but the "old" cellar which was the original foundation of the house. Not a tile but a hard-packed dirt floor, low ceiling festooned with cobwebs, smell of rot, decay. No windows—of course. And here, a "crawl space" burrowing into the very earth where a luckless workman might have to crawl if the cellar flooded in a heavy rainstorm and one of the sump pumps had broken.

You would need a flashlight there. No lights to switch on overhead.

You would need to stoop, you could not stand up straight.

Old stone cistern, not used for decades. Dank smell of the deaths of tiny creatures and their skeletons disarticulated and lost in the earth.

Jeering voices, laughter. Reaching a crescendo in the thaw of April when the dripping began outside my window.

Her windows, facing the lake. Just a degree or two colder on that side of the house so that the icicles outside my windows always began to thaw first. Then to drip faster-faster so I lay at night grinding my teeth.

First, the dripping. Then, the jeering voices from below. *The ugly one! The left-behind one! Georg-ene . . .*

Near-inaudible at first like a faint radio station and then louder by degrees until in my room two floors above I lay awake interminable nights unable to not hear it, through the walls I heard, through the damned furnace vent I heard it. Barefoot on the hardwood floor I felt the vibrations, thrumming-shuddering that made my heart beat harder.

Soon then, high-pitched cries through the floorboards that tore at my nerves like wires strung unbearably tight.

Almost I could see the thing's eyes in the perpetual twilight of my room with a single lamp burning (for even at my age I retained a childish fear of the dark, to this very day I require a "night-light" in my room), smell the stink of the creature's terror, which was like the scent of fresh blood in my nostrils, and would not let me sleep. If they had let me sleep! And so in the night at last making my way down the back stairs barefoot and trembling and along the (lightless) corridor past the shut door of the housekeeper's room to the cellar door at the rear of the old house in silence unerring like a sleepwalker and with the audacity and recklessness of the sleepwalker who understands that, so long as the trance of sleep is upon her, she cannot be harmed, she is suffused with great and terrible powers, and how fortunate it was, the door to Lena's room was shut, in her bed Lena slept oblivious of the angel of death passing so closely by her, for if the housekeeper had surprised me, if the foolish old woman had attempted to deter me, what might have happened to Lena, what might have come crashing down on Lena's head, crushing her skull I could not have prevented, whispering *Thank you God, thank you God for sparing Lena* as, descending the cellar stairs, no need to switch on the light, for *the hideous thing in the wall*, the creature, its skittering claws, high-pitched jeering laughter drew me to it unerring.

At the foot of the stairs hunched and crouching. So *she* discovered me in a sudden splash of light.

Gigi what on earth? Is that you?

Gigi you are so—silly . . .

Laughing, which was a mistake. Always a mistake to laugh at G.

Trying to explain to her, the voices, the laughter, the old cellar, the crawl space, the thing that crouched there. Smell of the creature's droppings in the dirt floor. *Hideous thing*, you could not see its face. And her saying *silly, there's nothing. I'll show you there's nothing there.*

The shovel in my hands, one of those heavy iron shovels with a wooden handle worn smooth by decades, to defend myself I struck, struck and struck eyes shut against the creature's terrified face, slamming the flat side of the shovel against its head again, again and again until the hair was clotted with blood and the cries became whimpers, then ceased.

A final convulsion. Daring to open my eyes but the thing was unrecognizable, and unmoving.

On my knees in the earthen floor. Had not wept like this in years, such relief.

Such a weight, lifted! The pressure of the hot mad lava erupting out of the volcano, at last.

Thank you God. Delivered from mine enemies. Amen.

Grunting I would drag it into the old cellar. And into the crawl space. Hours are required. Hours, days. Weeks and years. With the bloody-haired shovel digging a shallow grave for that was the most I could manage, in this cramped space. And having to hunch over for I could not stand upright. Sorrow, which is the dark side of joy. As much of a grave as required to hide the broken bleeding *thing.*

22

Thaw. With a jolt waking. Rapid-fire dripping outside the window.

In the groggy confusion, malaise of *aftersleep* not knowing at first where I am.

Palms of my hands aching, gritty. Dried sweat on my forehead, at the nape of my neck where my hair is clotted, snarled. Rivulets of sweat running down my sides as I lie on my back struggling to breathe like a hog that has rolled onto its back unable to right itself for the benumbed thickness of its limbs.

And how quiet the house. Except for the icicles dripping. For it is the twilight before dawn. For the others are sleeping. Surely *she* is sleeping. For *it has not happened yet.*

(Has it?)

23

The Story of the Scar. Never was the story told to me and yet I knew it by heart. I knew it as if it had been my own story. I knew it from M.'s silence, which was an angry silence. I knew it from the shiny little scar on M.'s face that winked and squinted if you looked at it too long like a furtive eye. I knew it because it *had not* happened to me. I knew it because no man had ever followed me in the early dusk after school when I was seventeen years old on my way to my piano lesson and no man had ever come up swiftly behind me and struck me so hard with his fist against the back of my head I fell without a cry, only a faint whimper of something like surprise—*Oh why* . . . And no man had ever dragged me along the ground by my ankles on my stomach, on my face scraping raw against filthy concrete and helpless to scream though not far away was a busy thoroughfare, traffic hurtling past like thunder; and no man had ever cursed me, and put his hands on me in a rage, and torn at my clothing, and afterward there were leaves and twigs in my hair and dirt stuffed into my mouth to gag me and a bleeding face like a Hallowe'en mask. *None of this had ever happened to me and yet I knew. I was not a beautiful girl of seventeen and I would never be a beautiful girl of seventeen and yet I knew, I rejoiced in what I knew because beauty deserves to be punished because beauty is selfish. Because beauty should be dragged by its ankles and its face scraped raw. Because beauty is not a child with a wrong-sized "bite" that had to be surgically corrected and beauty is not a mouth too crowded with teeth for the lips to close or a forehead low like an orangutan's or coarse curly hair and a nose shiny as a bugle or eyes that appear mismatched or "crossed" though they are staring straight at you seething in contempt.*

24

Not Really, Not Seriously Assaulted. This had been a time before Mother died. A time so long-ago G. was but a young child, ten years old.

This time long-ago when my sister returned home after dark crying, disheveled and her face bleeding, by which time Mother was in an agitated state for Marguerite had failed to appear at her piano teacher's house and the piano teacher called our home to ask where she was, if she was coming, lessons had to be canceled forty-eight hours ahead of time or the usual fee was expected, and so Mother was annoyed but also frightened, her first impulse was to scold, shocked to see what a sight M. was with torn and filthy clothing, and her hair matted, and her face bleeding, quickly Mother pulled M. out of my

sight where I was gaping and gawking for (of course) I'd
been waiting for Marguerite to come home peering out
a window into the rain dusk; Mother pulled Marguerite
into a downstairs bathroom and locked the door, ran cold
water with which to rinse M.'s bleeding face, telling M. to
please stop crying, not to become hysterical, not to disturb
Father (who was home, and in his office at the rear of the
house), and not to call attention to herself, what on earth
had she done to herself Mother demanded; and M. said
that a man had "hurt" her—a man had "put his hands on
her" and "dragged her" along the ground—and told her he
would "hurt her worse" if she told anyone; and he would
hurt her family too. She had not seen his face clearly but
he was an "adult man"—"a big man"—"a white man"—he
had seemed angry with her as if he knew her or (maybe)
he knew Father; (maybe) he'd been watching her, waiting
for her crossing the park to the piano teacher's house; and
Mother cried, what a thing to say!—of course this person
didn't know Father, that was ridiculous, how would Father
know such riffraff, M. should never make such an accusa-
tion like that again. And Mother washed M.'s face tenderly.
And Mother gave M. one of her pale pink lozenge-pills to
"calm her nerves"; and Mother ran a hot bath for M., in
her own bathroom upstairs with the claw-footed tub, and
examined M. without her clothes so far as M. would allow

her for M. was crying, wincing, pushing Mother's hands away, still agitated and upset despite the lozenge-pill.

After M. soaked in hot water for a half hour she became drowsy, and ceased whimpering, and Mother helped her climb out of the deep claw-footed tub, dried her tenderly in one of Mother's enormous thick bath towels, and put a bandage over the bleeding wound in M.'s face, took some time to brush briars and dirt out of her damp hair; led her like a young child to lie down on Mother's bed with a quilt over her admonishing her to *try to sleep*.

All of this, or much of this, Mother relayed to Father. What a lot of fuss! This *bad thing* that had happened to their beautiful daughter.

All this I knew, don't ask how. Nothing happened or happens in our household that *I do not know. For I do.*

Should they take M. to a doctor?—should they call the police?

Or—should they spare M. the further upset, by *keeping it quiet*?

At this time Father had an office in Aurora, upstairs over one of his Main Street properties. Through the weekdays, sometimes until Saturday noon, Father was at work. What the exact nature of Father's work was, we did not know, for Father was mysterious laying his forefinger against his nose saying *Money begats money, in the right hands*. He summoned one of his most trusted attorneys, a close friend from college days at Cornell, he and the attorney and Mother discussed the situation at length for it was "not an easy call"—as Father said: for, as Mother said, M. had not been *really, seriously assaulted*—(by which was meant: M. had not been *raped*)—so far as Mother could see; and by M.'s account, the man had been interrupted by someone or something, or had changed his mind, releasing her and running away, leaving her limp and unresisting on the walkway, now on her back, part naked, arms and legs helplessly outflung and her breathing so short, she could not call out for help.

In this way deciding to *keep the matter to themselves*.

To spare M. To protect M. Nothing in the newspaper!— Father was determined.

Protecting their (beautiful) (honor-roll) daughter. Protecting the family name.

For one thing—the "main thing": as the attorney explained—M. had been "roughed up" but had not been "raped."

"Rape" has but one legal meaning and, it seemed, the man had not "raped" M., he had not even "molested" M. with his fingers, or so Mother claimed.

Yes, he had "done things" to her, that was clear. He had said "terrible things" to her—and he had "threatened her."

But lacking witnesses it would be difficult to prove (exactly) what he'd done.

And M. had not wanted to be taken to a doctor. Excitable, and upset, stammering *No no no.*

Admitting that she hadn't seen her attacker's face. It would be impossible to identify him. And the humiliation, and the shame, and "people talking" at her school, that would be like a stain on clothing, a permanent stain, worse than an actual scar.

For M. was one of the popular girls at Aurora High School. Pretty, popular, a class officer, active in many clubs, expected to be admitted to an excellent college. Not Aurora College where her mother had gone, and several of her relatives, but Cornell perhaps, or Vassar, or Amherst.

M. acknowledged that she had not been seriously injured. M. acknowledged, she had not been *really, badly hurt*—by which M. meant, without saying the actual, ugly word, she had not been *raped.*

Just beaten, and dragged along the pavement, and her face scraped raw, and her teeth bloodied. Disgusting things he'd said to her, she would wish she could kill him, murder him. If she'd had a knife. If she'd had a knife and the courage to use it.

But—*it hadn't been the very worst. No.*

Over a period of days, the issue was decided. Quietly they'd talked to M.

The younger sister G. had not been told. Not a word!

Yet, the younger sister G. knew. All.

To be a (greedy, voracious) younger sister is to know all.

Aurora Police were not called. No appointment was made to bring M. to our family doctor. No report of an "assault" was ever made. No record, the last thing you want in a small town is anything like a *record,* a *reputation.* Father's attorney did not have to explain to Father and Mother nor to M. herself, M. was an intelligent girl, she understood.

Worse scars than a near-invisible shiny scar on her face that looked, close-up, in a certain sort of light, like a teardrop.

25

Passing. At Cornell M. would pledge Kappa Kappa Gamma, one of the preeminent sororities on campus.

Why?—she'd laughed saying just to see if I could do it. If I could pass for a Kappa.

A teardrop scar is easily disguised by makeup, all sorority girls wear makeup, most common popular disguise of all.

26

At the Piano. After the assault in the park that (officially) had not occurred when M. was a junior in high school, M. refused to return to piano lessons. Refused to return to the brownstone facing the park where, on the ground-floor, garden-level her piano teacher had met with her each Thursday after school.

(It may have been when M. began to call herself "M."—not "Marguerite." As she would make it a fetish, as an artist, to nullify all suggestions of sex, gender, in her work, and became furious if, in reviews of her sculptures, her name was given as "Marguerite Fulmer" and not "M. Fulmer.")

Irrationally, to our parents' dismay, M. refused to agree to piano lessons with another instructor saying she'd come to hate the very sound of a piano, the distinctive sharp smell of a piano. The very word *piano* made her gag!—she said. She threw out her lesson books but Mother retrieved them from the trash, brushed them off and gave them to me and for a few months at the age of ten I took piano lessons, not with M.'s teacher (who was the best piano teacher in town) but with a mediocre instructor at my grade school, practicing my lessons when M. wasn't in the house for M. could not bear to hear my stumbling efforts at the keyboard; but soon it became clear that M.'s younger sister G. had no talent for piano, no talent for music, she could not "count beats"—could not hear when she struck a wrong note—flat, sharp; and so at the piano often I would drum the keys with my fists; at the Steinway spinet which had originally been the property of great-great-grandparents of M.'s and mine which had a cherrywood veneer and smelled of a certain kind of furniture polish that roused me to rage drumming with my fists at the black keys in particular which vexed me until some of them became stuck and did not play as they had for my sister M. and so one day Mother came up silently behind me and seized my fists to stop their drumming, closed the keyboard, and brought my piano lessons to an abrupt end with a single word uttered in disgust—*Enough*.

102

And soon then, the Steinway spinet was locked. And ever after, the Steinway spinet was avoided, in a corner of the living room. To this day, no doubt badly out of tune, its formerly beautiful cherrywood dried and warped, mice nesting in its frayed strings and a patina of dust covering its surface, the piano has remained locked and silent and protected from the brutal assaults of a malevolent child's fists.

27

The Haunting. Soon after M. left us it began to happen. When I was alone. On a street in town. On my way to the grocery. The drugstore. The Mill Street Post Office.

Glancing up squinting and seeing—*her.*

M., just turning a corner. M., crossing an intersection, back to me. M., reflected in a store window staring contemptuously at me.

Strangely, I did not ever see M. with another person: always, M. was *alone.*

Nor did I see M. in a vehicle, either driving or as a passenger.

Of course, these sightings of M. were not really *of* M. Rather, strangers who resembled my sister; or, in some cases, didn't really resemble M. much at all, when

I recovered enough from my shock to look closely at them.

Often too, in months to come when I began walking (alone) on Drumlin Road, and on the hilly campus of the women's college, and in the old Aurora cemetery (in which the earliest Fulmers were buried beneath weatherworn tombstones tilted in the soil, thin as playing cards) on gusty days in particular I would see, or imagine that I saw, M. at a little distance from me, but usually with her back to me, or in profile; most frequently, inside the post office, where I was trapped behind the counter like a pig herded to slaughter, in the late afternoon just before closing there came the door pushed open with unusual force as if blown by the wind, a blurred presence entering, the visceral shock of seeing past the bland pie-face of a customer at the counter—*her face* . . .

"Ma'am, are you all right?"—the pie-face called sharply to me seeing that I seemed to be fainting, could not remain upright falling, grabbing blindly at something to break my fall, hold myself up, whimpering in fright as heavily I fell to the not-clean linoleum floor behind the counter clutching at sheets of first class stamps crumpled in a sweaty fist.

28

"Farewell Note."

> Dear Father,
> Please forgive me.
> I will explain my selfish behavior one day.
> Your daughter
> Marguerite

(*Selfish* was not chosen lightly but with much care and precision. For virtually everything in M.'s life was, indeed, examined from an objective perspective, *selfish*.)

This laconic note, hand-printed, in blue ink, I took the liberty of composing on a sheet of white construction paper belonging to M., on the day following the afternoon when I fell in a dead faint behind the counter at the post office and was revived only by a (busybody) co-worker kneeling beside me pressing paper towels soaked in luke-warm water against my burning face; and urged to leave as soon as I could walk unassisted, though twenty-five more minutes remained of my workday.

Imagined as a therapeutic undertaking, to alleviate Father's anxiety, which was exacerbating my own: to suggest that M. was, not a victim of a brutal abduction, but a "voluntary absentee."

(For Father too had begun to speak of "seeing" M. in town, at a distance; always with a feeling of shock and disbelief that did not subside for hours afterward.)

There was another reason for this stratagem: after a brief merciful period of time during which I had ceased to think of her at all the shameless *astrological psychic voyager* Mildred Pfeiffer had reasserted herself, daring to leave a note for me, with Lena, indicating that she had "valuable, priceless" information about M., to give me.

(Of which, more later.)

Hours of practice were required for me to master just M.'s signature, the only part of the note I dared to write in her hand.

Block-printing was something that M. might have done, in fact. In mimicry of an "artistic" font.

Later, rereading the note for the dozenth time, I decided
to add a date beneath the signature—

11 April 1991

—using the French way of dating, as it was M.'s way, one
of her affectations.

In this way hoping to allay Father's fears: that Father
would cease grieving for M., obsessing over M., accept
the fact that M. was gone (voluntarily) from Aurora, and
get on with his life.

Yes, and turn his fatherly attentions to *me*, his (other)
daughter.

And that the *astrological psychic voyager would leave me alone.*

◆

"No. Better not."

So I concluded, reluctantly.

Though the note was, in my opinion, a masterpiece of
brevity, and though I agonized for days over "discovering"
it amid M.'s papers in her room, I decided finally not to
bring it to Father after all.

Not because it was a forged document but rather that
it might be exposed as a *forged document* by detectives

suspicious of my finding it among M.'s things so many weeks after she'd disappeared.

Also, if the letter was addressed to Father, why wasn't it left for Father to find?—detectives were likely to ask. And maybe it was a giveaway, that I'd signed only M.'s name, and did not attempt to mimic her handwriting for the rest of the note.

"Absolutely no! *Not.*"

Father might have been relieved to think that M. had not been abducted and murdered but still, Father would have been upset, and would have notified the Aurora police; in turn, the Aurora police would have consulted the state police to provide them a forensic handwriting expert to determine if this note had really been written by M. Though I was fairly confident in my ability to deceive the experts, I was not one hundred percent confident, and could not risk being caught. And so I ripped up the very note I'd labored over for hours reasoning, like Falstaff, that discretion is the better part of valor.

Did not dare risk. Foolish risk. Unnecessary risk.

"Forging a note"—the fools would naturally suspect me *of having something to do with M.'s disappearance.*

29

"Voyager." How could it be explained, in early July 1991, approximately three months after the (alleged) disappearance of my sister Marguerite, the "psychic voyager" Mildred Pfeiffer herself disappeared?

So it was said. Claimed. *I* knew nothing of Pfeiffer firsthand, *I* had never set eyes upon the woman.

After I'd written my polite letter to her, and did not hear from her, I'd assumed, naively, that the woman had decided not to pursue the issue; that, if she'd hoped for some sort of financial reward from Father, and/or sensational publicity for herself in the less discerning media, she'd realized her error; but in this, in trusting to the good will of the other, I was mistaken.

For it began to be reported to me by relatives, and by friends of Father's, and even by colleagues of M.'s at the college whom the grotesque woman was pursuing, that Mildred Pfeiffer wasn't giving up so easily; and that I had underestimated her malevolent energy, for now she was "demanding" not only that she speak with Father and me but that she be involved in the police investigation.

For, it seemed, Pfeiffer was becoming impatient with the investigation, now in the hands of New York State detectives, with headquarters in Albany, whom she could not approach as easily as she could approach Aurora police.

It was Pfeiffer's demand that M.'s family—that is, Father and I—provide her with "intimate clothing" of M.'s, to allow her to "see" more clearly where M. was.

Needless to say, we refused to concede. The indignity!

All too often, Denise called me: "Georgene, have you *heard*?" The glee in my cousin's voice, the pretense of solicitude in her manner, set my teeth on edge; but I did not want to give Denise the satisfaction of knowing how upsetting her calls were to me.

In early July, to inform me that Pfeiffer was scheduled to be interviewed on WYIT, an Ithaca television station.

"Isn't that awful, Georgene? Can you imagine? Why would a reputable TV station invite someone like this?

111

With her claim that Marguerite isn't 'missing'—but in some way, I don't know how, here in Aurora, in hiding . . ."

Trying not to exclaim with vexation, fury. Trying to keep my voice level.

"Is that what she's claiming now, that Marguerite is 'in hiding'?"

"We're not sure. She's sounding crazier all the time. She's always hinting that she knows more than she can say. She was telling us—'Marguerite Fulmer is "missing" close to home. . .'"

"What do you mean, Denise, telling 'us'? Are you listening to this person? You haven't invited Pfeiffer into your house again, have you?"

"Not exactly, Georgene. I wouldn't say 'invited.' She just—shows up. She's accumulating a little entourage of Aurora residents who seem to believe her, or who are intrigued by her. Aunt Faye—you know, she's always been a little batty—is actually thinking of hiring Pfeiffer to make contact with Uncle Dave—Aunt Faye is convinced that Uncle Dave died with bank accounts no one knew about, she's always claimed that lots of money seemed to be missing when he . . ."

Biting my lower lip to keep from screaming into Denise's ear. Knowing that however calmly I spoke Denise would exaggerate my response and repeat it endlessly, to entertain.

"Denise, I think I'm going to have to hang up now. Father is calling me. . . ."

"Well! All right, Georgene. I just thought you would like to know."

"Thank you, Denise! When is this interview scheduled, do you know?"

"I think next week sometime. Midweek. It's the 'Chrissy Sheldon Hour'—you know, a hodgepodge of interviews, just after the evening news."

"Well, I will make sure that Father and I *do not watch*."

Managing to laugh gently, wryly. To assure Denise that none of this was truly upsetting to me, though to be regretted.

". . . just sorry, that poor Marguerite's name is being used like this," Denise said, as if reluctant to cease tormenting me. "I really think that, if you or Father pursued it, Pfeiffer would back away from the claims, if, you know, you offered her an incentive. . . ."

"Do you mean blackmail, Denise?"

"Well, I guess—yes. She's serious about the astrology but she's also hoping for some financial reward, I think. Your father did offer fifty thousand dollars which no one has claimed yet."

"Fifty thousand dollars is an incentive, yes. I hope you aren't suggesting that Father and I capitulate to blackmail, Denise."

"Oh no! Not at all. I'm sure that Pfeiffer would settle for much less than fifty thousand. Probably one thousand would be enough."

"Did she tell you that, Denise?"

"What? Did she *tell me* that? Of course not! I am hardly on speaking terms with this woman, I assure you."

"But you seem to know a lot about her. Much more than anyone else knows."

"Well—she is a colorful 'eccentric,' I suppose. She doesn't live so far from us, actually—down the hill. That ramshackle old Tudor with the moss growing on the slate roof. You know, by Niagara Street."

"Really, Denise! Have you visited her there?" (How calm I was being! Even, indeed, smiling, with clenched teeth.)

"Certainly not, Georgene. Why on earth would I visit—*her*. A mentally ill person . . ."

"Of course, Denise: you would not. None of us would. And now—I have to leave. *Father? I'll be right there.*"

Lifting my voice, as if Father were calling for me.

Quietly hanging up the phone. And damned proud of myself, neither Denise nor Mildred Pfieffer had broken my spirit, though both were trying.

30

The Disappeared. In the history of the United States an incalculable number of persons have disappeared: in the first decades of the twenty-first century, approximately 600,000 annually.

An astounding statistic! I would never have believed it except I have double-, indeed triple-checked, in the Cayuga County library.

Of these 600,000, approximately 90,000 are never found.

Of the approximate 510,000 that return, one-half return voluntarily, and one-half are returned by authorities.

Of those voluntarily missing, who then return, a considerable number are mentally unstable. "I just wanted to see if someone would ask if I was okay when I returned"—a woman who'd gone missing for several weeks told police.

(But did anyone inquire if this hapless woman *was* okay? That information isn't given.)

A considerable number of younger missing females are found to have been sexually abused, often by residents in their households; of these, an entire category is labeled *runaway*, and likely to be processed in county juvenile facilities rather than returned to their households.

One fact struck me: of those who return voluntarily, 97% return within two weeks.

With each passing week, it is less likely that the *missing* will return.

♦

Twenty-two years ago, in 1991, more than 540,000 persons disappeared in the United States, of whom (just) one was my sister Marguerite Fulmer.

In that year, more than 3,000 unidentified bodies were discovered.

Of these, one-quarter were female, and of these, at least two-thirds appeared to be victims of sexual violence whose bodies bore the evidence of that violence.

In every year, the number of missing persons under the age of twenty-one is far greater than over; and in every year, the number of missing males of all ages surpasses the number of missing females of all ages.

Like M. they leave their home—for work, for school—on a seemingly ordinary morning and are never found again. They set out upon brief journeys but never reach their destinations.

They drive away in their own vehicles, or board buses, trains, airplanes. They walk. They bicycle. They hike in remote places. (If hiking with others they may simply "disappear" on the trail.) They leave to meet a friend—and never show up. They step outside their residences to breathe the night air, or to smoke a cigarette—and never return. They call to a spouse that they are driving to the drug store and will be right back—but they are never *right back*.

Often, they take nothing with them, of which anyone is aware. They step "off the face of the earth."

If they withdraw money from a bank it's clear that they are *voluntary absentees*—and police will not search for them. But many do not withdraw money, as they do not pack suitcases, prepare for a trip. They don't take a change of clothes, a toothbrush. Like M., they leave no farewell note, they give no "sign."

Where before M.'s disappearance I took virtually no interest in "news"—and rarely subjected to myself to

TV news programs, as I have better things to do with my time than gape at a screen manufactured in the service of selling gullible consumers useless merchandise and services—after M.'s disappearance I fell into the anxiety-producing habit of watching nightly news, with Father seated in his adjustable leather chair close by like a lethargic King Lear, sipping Scotch whisky.

In the very week of M.'s disappearance residents of Cheektowaga, White Plains, and Lake George (all New York State) also disappeared under mysterious circumstances: a pattern? sheer coincidence?

The *psychic voyager* would probably say "pattern." The skeptic would probably say "coincidence."

Certainly it had to be a coincidence that the Cheektowaga resident, a wife and mother in her early thirties, bearing a superficial (blond) resemblance to M., disappeared in her Ford station wagon on the afternoon of April 11, having said that she was going grocery shopping; after twenty-four hours there was no trace of the mother of two young children, nor of her station wagon. (Cheektowaga is a moderately affluent suburb of Buffalo, one hundred fifty miles to the west from Aurora.)

In White Plains, two hundred fifty miles east and south from Aurora, a nineteen-year-old college student disappeared somewhere, on foot, between the Vassar campus and the house she rented with several other young women, a half mile away; after thirty-six hours, she too was still missing.

At Lake George, a forty-six-year-old husband and father, a year-round resident at the lake, took out a small outboard motorboat to fish alone at dawn, on a mildly windy morning; hours later the boat was sighted empty and drifting. . . . Fishing equipment, water bottle, and other items left behind. (Lake George Marine Patrol searched the lake near the drifting boat, to a depth of one hundred seventy feet, but no body was found.)

So far as I know, none of these missing persons was ever found.

And then, so strangely, one might say *ironically*: on July 7, 1991, on the very eve of her scheduled interview with the TV hostess Chrissy Sheldon, the shameless *psychic voyager* Mildred Pfeiffer herself "disappeared"—"vanished off the face of the earth."

This disappearance of a local resident, unlike Marguerite's disappearance, warranted a much smaller front-page column of print in the *Aurora Journal*: *Aurora "Psychic" Reported Missing*. The accompanying photograph was of a squinting cat-faced woman of about fifty identified as a longtime resident of Lakeview Avenue, living with her schoolteacher-sister and their elderly mother; according to the mother, Mildred Pfeiffer had received a telephone call in the late afternoon of July 7, and left the house immediately—"Looking like she was excited about who she was meeting."

Unfortunately, if Mildred Pfeiffer had told her mother where she was going, whom she was meeting, the elderly woman was too agitated to remember, and a search of Mildred's things did not turn up any clue.

And so, Mildred Pfeiffer, like Marguerite Fulmer, took her place among that mysterious category of *missing persons* who do not return, are not returned by authorities, but remain *missing* forever.

◆

"Georgene! Did you *see*—? In the *Journal*—?"

Excitedly, voice quivering, Denise called me, as I knew she would, with news of the *psychic voyager*; and so I was prepared to say coolly *No*.

"You know I don't read the *Journal*, Denise, if I can avoid it. Especially when they publish such stupid things about Marguerite and our family. I am going to hang up now."

"But, Georgene—"

"Good*bye*, Denise. Please don't call again."

◆

So I came to see that my (beautiful) (doomed) sister was but a figure in a pattern, not singular or unique, as we (who loved her) believed her to be.

For, each year a certain number of Americans *must disappear*, to make up the statistics, which do not vary much.

And how strange *that is*! Could there be a year when *no one at all* disappears? Why was this not likely?

Improbable? But not impossible?

By the fall of 1991, when M. had been gone for five months, "sightings" of her had diminished dramatically. We heard less frequently from the (intrusive) detectives in Albany, and nothing at all from the (incompetent) detectives in Aurora. I paid a young boy-cousin to drive me to Ithaca on the far side of the lake, to the Cayuga County Public Library where I spent fascinated hours researching *missing persons*, including the infamous Judge Joseph Crater who'd vanished, allegedly, after having stepped into a taxi on West 45th Street, Manhattan, on August 6, 1930. (The circumstances of Judge Crater's disappearance were very different from those of my sister's disappearance for, as it turned out, Crater had been involved in various political schemes, and was soon to be exposed as corrupt in the press; and he'd left a touching note for his wife: *Am very weary. Love, Joe.*)

As we know, Judge Crater was never found. Nor did anyone ever unearth a single clue to his disappearance, at least officially.

Similarly, Jimmy Hoffa. Like Crater, a man involved with criminals, no doubt executed and his remains hidden—a different sort of mystery since there are certainly people who know where the *missing person* is.

The most famous of American *missing persons* remains Amelia Earhart who'd disappeared when her plane crashed in the Pacific Ocean in 1937, when Earhart was thirty-nine: not really a mystery why she'd vanished, only just where.

It's the other category of *missing* that fascinates, because inexplicable: a fifty-year-old man in Seabury, Oregon, disappears on his way to work; his car is found on the shoulder of an interstate, abandoned: doors locked, keys on the driver's seat. A thirty-six-year-old woman in Larchmont, New York, disappears on her way home from a high school guidance counselors' conference; a forty-nine-year-old insurance salesman in Evanston, Illinois, disappears after having deposited a sizable amount of money in his checking account, an account that is never activated. . . . Occasionally there is a *double-missing*: a honeymoon couple hiking on a mountain trail in Yosemite, a mother and her young daughter in Rome, New York, never seen again after driving to a local mall to shop for back to school clothes. . . .

Unless the *missing person* is famous such cases are excitedly reported in local media, there is a flurry of interest, rewards may be offered, a "suspect" or two might be questioned, and then—nothing. . . . Dropping out of headlines is like dropping out of existence.

Sometimes, of course, the missing *are* found: as corpses.

Or, less likely, they are discovered alive, hundreds or thousands of miles away, living under different names, with forged documents and social security numbers, in fabricated second lives.

Exactly what Father believed, I was not sure. I did not like to question Father on subjects that agitated him. At times, Father seemed to be resigned to the melancholy knowledge that M. would never return; at other times, especially when he'd been drinking, a flush would enliven his face, his eyes would shine defiantly as he said, to anyone who might hear, often to me: "She *is* alive. I feel it. And *she will* come home. Someday."

To which I would only murmur sympathetically *Yes, Father.*

While thinking in angry dismay *Oh Father! Why, when you have* me?

PART II

PART II

31

Despicable. Of course, from the start there were despicable rumors circulated by despicable rumor-mongers. I have been reluctant to speak of these, as I have been reluctant to speak of the *psychic voyager.* (Who'd had at least the decency to "disappear" herself from our midst and not further sully my sister's reputation.)

Among these were rumors that M. had been "pregnant" —and had fled her hometown in shame.

Or, M. had been "pregnant, and had an abortion"—and had fled in shame; or, had died on the abortionist's table, and her body secretly buried.

(Why an abortion, in a civilized region of the United States, in 1991, would have so derailed my sister's life was never explained: M. was not an evangelical Christian or a Catholic, for whom abortion was a sin.)

Rumors that M. was "involved in drugs"—"had died of an overdose."

Rumors that M. had "eloped" with a man so unsuitable, so shameful, she could not bring herself to remain in Aurora with him.

Rumors that M. had been "involved with a married man"—and had fled Aurora out of unhappiness; or, had been murdered by the man, to protect his marriage.

The most persistent rumor was that, as a consequence of pregnancy, abortion, shameful love or thwarted love, or just run-of-the-mill suicidal depression, M. had taken her own life: wading out in the night into the lake behind our house, pockets weighed with stones like Virginia Woolf.

(At least this cruel rumor could be investigated: the county sheriff's department arranged for a diver to search the lake behind our house to a distance of several hundred feet. Indeed, skeletal remains of creatures were discovered amid the muck of the lake bottom but—*no human remains.*)

"Despicable!"—as Father would say. As soon as one rumor was discovered, and derisively discounted, another would flare up, like wildfire; and some of these rumors, I knew very well, originated with our relatives, especially those who'd always been envious of us, for having the most wealth of the Fulmers, and of M., for being the most accomplished of the younger generation of Fulmers.

The rumor that M. had been involved with a man, and may have been murdered by a lover, was eventually linked to a colleague of M.'s in the art school—the pretentious *artiste* who called himself "Elke."

Here was the most despicable person of all, of my entire acquaintance.

At first I'd had no idea who he was—a brazenly staring big-bellied man of about forty in paint-splattered coveralls, rudely approaching me when I went to M.'s studio on the afternoon of April 12, when M. had been missing for a full day.

"Excuse me: who are you?"

"I—I am Marguerite Fulmer's sister. . . ."

Trying to fit a key into the studio door, as the big-bellied man stared suspiciously at me.

Usually I am a match for a bully but in this case, having slept poorly the previous night, and being genuinely anxious about the situation, I found myself fumbling for words, even as I fumbled the key. By this time search parties had been looking for M. for hours, with nothing to report.

"*Her* sister! Really."

The big-bellied man seemed bemused. For, it's true, I do not bear much obvious resemblance to my older sister.

With annoying familiarity the man took the key from my fingers and deftly opened the door.

His name was "Elke," he said. His studio was just across the hall.

The way in which he pronounced "Elke" allowed me to know that this was a name of some distinction, which should impress me. But I am not so easily impressed.

If "Elke" had thrust out his hand to shake mine, I did not seem to notice. My face smarted from the bully's rudeness, I had no wish to encourage him.

Uninvited, Elke followed me into M.'s studio, which was a smaller space than I would have anticipated, though with a high ceiling and a skylight. Elke was saying that he'd tried to call Marguerite also, the day before. She'd missed a sculpting class and a meeting. The department was concerned about her. *He* was concerned about her.

Swaggering Elke was taller than I, by several inches. I am not a fragile woman but Elke outweighed me by thirty pounds at least. I saw how his beady-glittery reptilian eyes glanced about M.'s studio, a look of greed in his face.

"We had plans to go for a drink at the Inn after the meeting. We had something to discuss—a departmental issue."

A pause and then: "Well, a personal issue too."

To this startling remark, I made no reply. It did not occur to me at the time that it was probably a lie—I was in too confused a state to be thinking clearly.

"That's why I'm particularly concerned about Marguerite," Elke said, "—she would have called me to postpone our meeting, if she could. And so—if . . ."

His voice trailed off suggestively. I felt the hairs stir on the nape of my neck. There was something aggressively familiar in the way Elke pronounced my sister's name—as if he hadn't the right but was now claiming the right since there was no one to stop him.

And now I remembered that someone named "Elke" had called the previous day, and Father had spoken curtly with him. I remembered that M. had once remarked that she owed her position at Aurora College to the senior artist-in-residence who admired her work, a painter with a "controversial" reputation; if he hadn't wanted her, or had vigorously championed someone else, she would not have been appointed.

So, M. was "grateful" to Elke—possibly.

Had M. said anything further about this "senior artist"?—I could not recall.

Had they had some sort of closer relationship? I doubted an *intimate relationship*—bewhiskered big-bellied Elke could not have appealed to my fussy fastidious sister in the slightest.

131

It was annoying, how M. never confided in me her true feelings about Aurora College. She tended to speak positively, even enthusiastically, about most people with whom she was associated; she had an aversion, she'd said, to talking "behind people's backs." She'd never said a word—to me, at least—critical of her colleagues at Aurora College, surely an assortment of mediocre academics who'd failed to find positions at better colleges.

Such a hypocrite!—nothing that would ever be said about *me*.

True, Aurora College had a "prestigious" reputation in the category of small liberal arts colleges for women, especially in New York State; but that was not saying much, surely. It was altogether normal to make snide, amusing comments about co-workers, behind their backs, as we did routinely at the post office; it was dishonest of M. to be so reticent about her fellow artists at Aurora. Certainly self-aggrandizing "Elke" would have drawn her derision: the swaggering "macho" male, not young, vain and pompous, graying whiskers sprouting from his heavy jaws, breath thick, audible. His coarse gray hair fell in waves to his shoulders though the crown of his head was gleaming-bald. On his thick, hairy left wrist he wore a Native American–looking braided leather bracelet, on his massive feet hiking boots. His fingernails were ridged with paint, dirt. And those ridiculous paint-splattered coveralls! My nostrils pinched: Elke smelled of his body.

"You are—an older sister of Marguerite's?"

"No. I am not."

Stung by the rude query. Wanting to tell the fool that I was *six years younger* than Marguerite but I was too dignified to explain.

"Oh hey—sorry." Elke sounded more amused than embarrassed.

Badly I'd hoped to be alone to search M.'s studio—as I'd been alone, fortunately, to search M.'s room before detectives barged into our house and searched it; if there was anything that might be embarrassing to M., or to our family, I had to get my hands on it, immediately. (A diary, a journal?) (What might be in it, in theory, I had no idea. That is not how my mind works. As a daughter of Milton Fulmer my priority was to protect him from any sort of upset.)

But there was no way to avoid Elke. I could not order him out of my sister's studio—this was not a private studio but a space in the arts college where Elke had a position of authority. His manner was bossy, proprietary. He was particularly fixated on M.'s uncompleted sculptures: curious geometrical shapes in vivid-white rock resembling slightly deformed heads with faint hieroglyphic marks that might have been facial features, displayed on

133

a cluttered workbench. The largest was three feet high and about three feet in circumference, the smallest was the size of an actual human, adult head. There was something both eerie and touching about these sculptures. I hated how Elke drew his fingers over them with a mocking sort of familiarity, like a man stroking a dog's head.

"Your sister has a wonderfully perverse imagination. Most people can't decode it—*I* can."

Has. It occurred to me that Elke was deliberately using the present tense to signal that he believed that M. was still living.

(Of course, at this time M. had scarcely been missing a day.)

"Really!" Coolly I meant to ignore Elke, and to allow him to know my intention.

"Marguerite was surprised, when I first met her, and talked to her about her art—the 'secret mission' of her art. So different from my own: in fact, antithetical."

Antithetical was pronounced with a certain gravity. Possibly, Elke thought that I might not know the meaning of the word.

"Are you familiar with my work, Ms. Fulmer? My 'portraits'?"

"No, I'm afraid not, Mr. Elke. I don't get over here to the college often."

How funny—*Mr. Elke*. Of course, my expression was
dead-serious, polite.

"My work—my paintings—are quite well known," Elke
said, annoyed, "—not just here at the college. You've surely
seen them in Aurora—in the Inn, at the library, in private
homes..."

"I don't believe so, Mr. Elke. No."

"I am not 'Mr. Elke'—just call me 'Elke.'"

"'El-ke.'"

"*Elke.*"

"Do you mean, like the animal? A larger species of
moose?"

With the most sincere-sounding naivete I spoke. The
pompous *artiste* had no idea how I was laughing at him,
in silence.

"As I said, my work is antithetical to Marguerite's.
We've had some pretty intense discussions about art.
She's a classicist—a formalist—out of timidity, a fear of
the body; in her case, the female body. Which is why she
insists upon exhibiting as 'M. Fulmer'—a sexless name.
Of course she denies it. While I—I confront 'bodily
decrepitude' pitilessly in my work—my 'portraits of
mortality.'"

Now I was wondering if in fact I'd seen some of Elke's
paintings, on the walls in the Aurora library, where local

135

artists were exhibited. Human figures, nudes? Unsparing, macabre *nudes*?

If I'd seen, I'd probably glanced quickly away. Most of modern art seemed to me fraudulent and gimmicky, and "local artists" the most pathetic of all.

Of all categories of art, my least favorite is *nudes*.

"I wonder if Marguerite has spoken to you about me?"—now, more hesitantly Elke spoke, as if knowing how he was setting himself up for a rebuke.

How pathetic, I thought. How like Walter Lang. *Begging* to be humiliated.

"No. I don't think so. Not that I recall."

Matter-of-factly I replied, like a child intent upon telling the truth, with no notion of how the truth might hurt.

"Really?—no?" Elke was sounding wistful.

"Really, Mr. Elke—I mean, *Elke*. Really, *no*."

Elke stood uncertainly, as if air were leaking out of him. His beefy face looked wounded. The glittery reptilian eyes seemed harmless now, grown moist.

My instinct was to relent, just a little: "Marguerite rarely confides in me. Almost never about anyone in the arts school."

"Well—Marguerite and I are more than just colleagues, here. We are—strange as it sounds, since in other ways we are opposites—what you'd call 'soul mates.'"

"'What *I'd* call 'soul mates'?—no, I don't think so, Mr. Elke. I don't believe in anything so ridiculous as 'soul mates.'"

And especially not you, a "soul mate" of my beautiful sister! Absurd.

Elke was silent, brooding. Wanting to protest but thinking better of it.

He'd sized me up, perhaps: *sexless as a turnip, man-hater, immune and invulnerable.*

"Well. I hope that nothing has happened to Marguerite. . . . She didn't tell anyone where she might be going? You don't have any idea?"

"Excuse me, 'Elke,' but we've gone over all that with the police. My father and me. I'm very tired, and distraught, and not in a mood to talk to strangers about my missing sister."

"But I am not a stranger!—I'm a close friend of Marguerite's, I've tried to explain. Somewhat closer than 'friend' . . . And I'm a neighbor of yours, you and your family, Aurora is a small town."

Neighbor! Now, this was truly absurd. Homeowners on either side of our stately old English Tudor on Cayuga Avenue would not have claimed *neighborliness* with us, nor would we with them. Upper Cayuga Avenue was not a common *neighborhood.*

It was touching, how big-bellied bewhiskered Elke seemed hurt now, flummoxed. So a bully is easily wounded if you know his Achilles heel: his ego.

If I'd wished to relent just a bit, I might have asked to visit his studio, on my way out. I might have asked to see his "portraits of mortality." He would have liked that very much, he would have been flattered. But I do not flatter. I am not a nice person, so why pretend? I had not the slightest interest in this *artiste*'s art, nearly as little interest as I had in my sister's pretentious "classicism."

But I did envy M. this studio. A private work-space away from home. M.'s private life—her "secret mission." All that was *secret* in my sister, I deeply envied, and resented.

For my life has no secrets. Or, you could say that my secret is that I *have no life*.

Overhead the skylight yielded a bright light that fell vertically into the studio, illuminating the sculptures-in-progress on the workbench. Would she return, and complete them? If she did not return, would they be exhibited nonetheless, as M. Fulmer's "last work"?

If M. did not return, these uncompleted sculptures would become Father's property, I supposed. Father's, and mine.

If M. had not left a will leaving them elsewhere. As I was sure she had not.

For who, at the age of thirty, even thinks of a *last will &
testament*? Not M.!

One of the four studio walls was plate glass, overlooking a grassy hill and the college bell tower—an idyllic
scene, almost *too pretty*; the other walls were almost totally
covered in posters, sketches, diagrams, drawings, photographs. A large cork bulletin board was filled with
what appeared to be student work—sketches, drawings,
announcements of student events. There was a charming
naivete about these that set them apart from M.'s own
austere work.

Until now I had not really thought of M. as an art
instructor. I felt a stab of jealousy, that M.'s students would
know her in a way that I never had.

All young women, of course. Younger than me: girls. I
wondered if M. felt sisterly toward them, as she rarely felt
toward me. Patient, kindly. *Affectionate.*

You could be fooled. Give away your heart, fool! I wondered if Elke had given away *his.*

Reluctant to leave the studio Elke was examining the
bulletin board, pretending an interest in the student work.
While the man's paint-splattered coverall back was turned
I slipped an oversized, well-worn sketchbook into my bag,
which I'd found in a sliding drawer in the workbench.

A journal, possibly. A diary?

My heart beat rapidly in triumph. I wanted to laugh aloud, big-bellied Elke hadn't noticed a thing.

Time to leave M.'s studio. Lock up, and leave. Elke had no choice but to leave with me.

I had acquired the key to M.'s studio from the administrative assistant to the arts college director. I would return the key now, to the office on the first floor, as Elke awkwardly accompanied me on the stairs.

Even descending stairs, Elke was breathing audibly, through his mouth. The odor of his body wafted to my nostrils not unpleasantly, as if I'd grown accustomed to his smell. I felt a pang of sympathy for the man, scarcely forty years old, heart encased in fatty muscle straining to deliver oxygen to his brain.

On my way out of the college still Elke was following close beside me. I hoped that he wouldn't realize that I'd walked to the college, not driven; in his overbearing way he would ask if he could drive me home, and I would be reluctant to refuse, for I was indeed feeling tired, and distraught. My vigorous hike to the college by way of Drumlin Road, replicating M.'s steps, had been enough exercise for the day.

"Ms. Fulmer?—you didn't mention your name. . . ."

"No. I did not."

Such rudeness from a Fulmer, Elke couldn't quite grasp. Few can. You stare at me, and squint, and blink, and think—*She didn't just say that!*

"You didn't tell me your name, either—'Elke.' Your first name."

"I—it's—Howard. My birth name is Howard Strucht."

"So why do you call yourself 'Elke'?"

"'Elke' is my painter's name. Like a 'born-again' name. Closer to who I am."

Awkwardly Elke laughed. But I did not laugh with him.

"Well—Ms. Fulmer—I was wondering if I could come see you and your father sometime soon? Maybe tomorrow?"

"But why? I don't think so."

"Just to—talk. . . . About Marguerite."

Exasperated with him, impatient to be free of him, I said, sharply: "We are not in the habit of discussing Marguerite with strangers, I have tried to explain, Mr. El-ke. We do not have an 'open house' for strangers. If you know anything about my sister that the police should know, tell them. Don't tell *us*. We are overloaded with people telling us useless things, and we are very exhausted."

Pointedly I turned, and walked away from bewhiskered big-bellied panting "Howard Strucht." Dreading that he would follow me, with more wistful wheedling nonsense. But he did not.

Though calling after me, in a voice tinged with irony, like a hurt adolescent: "Well—goodbye! It was good to meet you."

I laughed to myself. I did not look back. Thinking—*No, it was not. But it's the best you can do.*

32

"Secret Mission." Returning home on foot, vexed to be forced to run a gauntlet to get into my own house past a noisy phalanx of reporters in the street, at least two TV camera crews, as well as gawkers kept at a distance by Aurora police officers, thank God for the six-foot wrought-iron fence around our property!—vulgar low-life strangers calling rude inquiries to me, whom I ignored with dignified disdain; then, inside the house, further vexed to see several familiar faces in the living room, with Father, including my callow cousin Denise, ostensibly here to give comfort, "commiserate"—meaning, as I knew well, to plumb the latest news about Marguerite, to be transformed into shameless gossip as soon as they left the premises.

"There she is!"—one of them murmured, even as Denise called out sharply, "Oh, Georgene—wait"—as I bounded up the staircase scowling back at her with a look of contempt impossible to misinterpret.

Do. Not. Dare. Follow. Me.

Very disappointed with Father. Very disappointed with Lena who dared to let these leeches into the house as soon as I'd left to hike over to the college.

In the morning, I would scold Lena. *Do not let* anyone in the house no matter who they are. No matter what Father says. To protect Father, we must be cautious.

Oh, I had to laugh, as M. would have laughed: how relatives from whom we hadn't heard in years were suddenly calling us, making a fuss over us, speaking in grave, urgent voices. Each of them with some absurd theory of where M. might be, what might have happened to her, recalling that *mysterious trouble* she'd had in her junior year in high school about which they knew little of substance except (of course!) it had to be, somehow, sexual; recalling *those years* she'd lived in New York City where (of course!) she'd surely made dangerous acquaintances, mingled with *the wrong sort* of people, a (secret, sordid) part of her life now reasserting itself in Aurora? Even relatives who'd been supportive of M. hadn't known what to think of her career as a sculptor: was it a *good thing*, something to be *proud of*, that M. had acquired renown outside her hometown or was it (somehow) worrisome, even scandalous, that M. had obviously mingled, in New York City, with suspicious persons like (for instance)—what was his name, that sleazy wig-wearing sham Pop Artist?—Andy Warhol? Mixed in with drugs, orgies. And (just possibly)—*lesbians* . . .

Much as I resented my sister, I more resented *them*. If I had to choose sides, no hesitation—I choose *my sister*.

Breathless in my room, shut the door and lock it!—in anticipation of Denise daring to come upstairs and knock.

As if, years ago, Denise had been a friend of mine, and not exclusively M.'s. As if, in fact, like our other cousins, she hadn't ignored me entirely, as soon as it became evident that I wasn't going to be an attractive girly-girl like their younger sisters.

Not only did I lock my door but, since locks in our house were not always secure, I dragged a chair over, to further secure it.

Sat on my bed, panting. My bed unmade for days. For I kept Lena out of my room. While M. was living at home I'd been obliged to conform to the laws of the household, allowing my room to be cleaned, vacuumed, spic-and-span as the rest of the house, now M. was gone immediately I was reverting to the pleasures of savagery—*Thank you, Lena. But I am perfectly capable of keeping my own room clean.*

Exhilarated from the theft, in the very presence of "Elke"; thinking that, if M. could have known, she'd been impressed with her younger sister's sangfroid, if furious at the violation of her privacy.

"But from now on, you have no more 'privacy.' You are a *missing person*."

Laughing, as I imagined the look of consternation in my sister's usually composed face.

Laughing, as I'd seen the look of surprise and shock in Denise's face downstairs: her realization that her young, insignificant cousin Georgene had ascended, in some way not yet clearly known, to a position of significance, a personage whom TV camera crews would call to, and reporters try to interview; none of which could have been predicted just a few days before.

"Yes, I have surprised you, haven't I? All of you."

My heart was beating rapidly. I was feeling giddy, almost gay. Not drunk—lightly intoxicated.

Though suffused with dread, too—that I had *gone too far*, finally.

And so, opening M.'s sketchbook, I was disappointed at first: seeing that it appeared to be nothing more than a random collection of sketches, an artist's journal of half-finished drawings, some of them very small and fine, in pencil; some, in charcoal; a few in pastel crayons, even a few watercolors executed quickly: charming, but slight.

Page after page of these. Occasional inserts of yellowed clippings—art exhibits, articles from *Art News*, *New Yorker*, *Fine Art Connoisseur*. (One of these articles, on Brancusi, was by *M. Fulmer* herself—I'd had no idea that M. published in such magazines; she had never shown me.)

Most of the drawn figures were abstract shapes, models for M.'s sculptures. Pale, anemic colors. Elegant, dreamlike. Yet precise. Yet—*boring*.

I understood Elke's impatience with my sister's work: a fear of the body, the "female body." As a sexual aggressor "elk" could only feel contempt for "m." The only serious criticism M. Fulmer received had been from occasional critics who chided her for neglecting, or failing, or refusing to explore more obvious, dramatic feminist subjects of the kind found in the eye-catching art of Marisol, Frida Kahlo, Cindy Sherman, Nan Goldin ("The Ballad of Sexual Dependency"). *For all her technical skill—which is considerable—M. Fulmer takes refuge in circumvention, shrinks from a political confrontation with the issues facing more courageous female artists of our time.*

Now, this annoyed me. Any attacks against *M. Fulmer* aroused my hostility. How dare they!—feminist fools.

M. hadn't deigned to defend herself, so far as I know. One of the clippings reported a "lively panel" of women artists, including *M. Fulmer*, at the Brooklyn Art Museum in October 1987, but the accompanying photo showed M. looking serene, composed, unthreatened amid the panel of dramatic-looking female *artistes*.

You could see, however, leafing through the sketchbook, that, to M., the abstract shapes *were* related to the female body, or (secret) expressions of it. As I looked more closely I could see how M. began with a "realistic" rendering of a nude human figure which was then increasingly abstracted as if its essence were being revealed while its surface details were expunged—there was something exciting in this, in fact, as if one could peer into the artist's brain. Several female breasts, each extraordinarily specific, with distinctive nipples, aureoles, imperfections in the skin were transfigured gradually into ovoid shapes in which only very faint features were retained, if one knew where to look, how to decode.

So too with female bellies, thighs, buttocks. Ankles, arms, elbows, shoulders. Less clear, shapes that might be female genitals—vagina, labia, vulva. Not a suggestion of pubic hair, however.

"That is the 'secret mission'—is it?"

As I leafed through the sketchbook I came to wonder if I was imagining these things. The artist loses herself in the specific, redeems herself in the abstract. I felt the tug of obsession, madness. *Why* did artists spend so much time staring, recording, composing, recomposing? What could be the possible motive?

Badly I wanted to cry "Enough! Stop."

Badly I wanted to tear out these pages at which M. had labored so fanatically, hour after hour.

Wondering why, if M. could draw so well, did she waste her time with these boring abstractions? It was remarkable, M. could draw something as ordinary as a woman's elbow, wrist, ankle, ear—and render it vivid, "alive." Yet—the drawing evolved into an abstraction in which the original was visible as a wraith might be visible, hovering inside the figure.

But there were landscape drawings in the sketchbook as well—very finely drawn, crosshatched, views of Cayuga Lake from M.'s windows. Delicate little watercolors, faded, the paper wrinkled and torn.

Moonlight on the lake, a flotilla of storm clouds, yew trees heaped with snow—these quick deft little drawings took my breath away, they were so exquisite . . .

Rough underbrush, in the no-man's-land behind our property. Eerily detailed, footprints and hoofprints in mud. A rabbit, paralyzed, wide-eyed, staring.

My sister was greatly gifted. It was all true—not exaggerated.

My mouth was dry. Compulsively I swallowed. I felt a wave of something like terror, that this gifted artist, my sister M., had gone *missing*. . . .

And how strange, what a treasure trove, this sketchbook with its battered cover! Some of the pages seemed to be water-stained.

I wondered if M.'s sketchbook contained her truest work, her most deeply felt work, while the icy-formal sculptures were the outer self, in disguise. A protective sort of armor, "classic" beauty.

But near the back of the sketchbook were rougher drawings, doodles. Caricatures of faces. Skillfully rendered as comic strips are rendered, with just a few telling lines. M. in a mischievous mood: the comic-strip character Popeye had been slightly modified, as a caricature of one of our older Fulmer uncles. Snobbish Aunt Ellen had been imagined as the grotesque Duchess from *Alice in Wonderland*, with an enormous head, sagging self-pitying face.

And here was a familiar, thuggish face—Elke? I laughed aloud, seeing how M. had captured the self-aggrandizing *artiste* with just a few deft strokes of a charcoal stick: pig-predator eyes, bulbous nose, whiskers both bristling and scanty, absurd hippie-hair cascading to his shoulders like a wig. Perfect!

How would Elke feel, knowing that M. perceived him like this?—not as a fellow artist but as a charlatan, with a male-predator glint in his eye.

A close friend of Marguerite's . . . Somewhat closer than a "friend."

What a fool! I wondered if Elke was in love with M.?—he'd certainly seemed to attach himself to me, and had been hard to shake off.

Next, I was shocked to come upon deft little portraits of Mother, Father.

There were many of these, miniatures. I wondered if M. had sketched them from life, observing our parents when they had no idea that they were being observed; or whether she recalled them so vividly in memory.

These were not caricatures, nor were they cruel. Thoughtfully rendered, like nineteenth-century cameos, as of persons no longer living.

Especially it was shocking, to see Mother so unexpectedly. The older, fatigued-looking woman who'd endured months of (futile, punishing) chemotherapy—which I'd tried to forget. But also the younger and more confident woman, quite a regal-looking woman, like a slightly thicker-faced Grace Kelly, smiling at the viewer.

Smiling at me? Is Mother smiling at—me? Forgiving me?

I hadn't forgiven *her*, for falling ill as she had. As if her illness had been a reproach to me. Childish, unfair, though I hadn't been a child but an older adolescent at the time.

Well—I am *not perfect*. I've never claimed to be.

Unlike M. who took a keen interest in our family background, as an anthropologist might take an interest in native subjects, I had never wanted to know much about my parents or grandparents.

That Hilda and Milton Fulmer were *my parents* was all that engaged me, essentially. I did not want to think that they'd had fully formed adult lives before me—before the idea of me. Especially I did not want to think that my parents had had romantic lives, erotic lives, had once been young, younger than I was now. I did not want to think—*I could not bear to think*—that they were (surely) disappointed in me.

The younger sister, the less "favored" sister. As in a fairy tale there had to be a Princess, and a Beggar-Maid. Nothing in between.

Of course, Mother had had her difficulties with Marguerite, who'd refused to conform to Mother's expectations. M., a *debutante*? She'd laughed in Mother's face at the mere thought.

Still, Mother had preferred M. to G., that went without saying. And Father—of course.

Clearly they'd loved M. far more than they'd loved me; that, I could not reasonably contest, as, in their places, I would have loved M. far more than G.

If one of the Fulmer daughters had to "go missing," how much preferable it would have been if it were G.!

M.'s portraits of Father were equally engaging, lifelike. Youthful, as he might have been in his thirties, stern-faced yet kindly, with the aristocratic "jut-jaw" I'd inherited from him, as well as the breadth of his forehead. Milton Fulmer's more attractive features, the set of his large intelligent eyes, the line of his "Roman" nose, I had not inherited, unfortunately.

And here was Father older, less confident. Lined cheeks, pouches of loose skin beneath his eyes. Still handsome, in a wan, worn way, like the older Clark Gable. Hair beginning to thin though snowy-white. *Widower*—it struck me. I had not thought of Father in that way, as a husband who'd lost his wife, until seeing him in M.'s sketchbook.

Indeed I never thought of Father as anyone other than *my father.* It made me very uncomfortable to think of him in relationship to someone else.

How frightening, to examine such portraits. To realize that each person, of the countless persons who live and had lived, is a distinct personality: unique.

Not related to *me* at all . . .

153

"Hello? Is that—Denise?" Sharply I called out, for I'd heard, or thought that I'd heard, a footfall outside my door.

Silence. No one.

"Is someone there? Hel-*lo*? Just go away, please."

But there was nothing. Evidently.

After a long moment, I began to relax: even pushy Denise wouldn't have dared follow me upstairs.

Seeing the way I'd glared at her. *Go to hell, Denise!*

Turning back to the sketchbook, I had to concede how remarkable it was, how M. had "captured" our parents. These were exquisite miniatures, more precious than snapshots. Tears dimmed my eyes. Indeed, I'd have liked to share them with someone, like Denise, except—well, *except that I hated Denise.*

As a girl I'd had some vague notion of being an *artiste*, too. Poetry—poetry seemed easier than anything else. Scribbling lines in a notebook, crude and unrevised like the Beats, for hadn't Allen Ginsberg extravagantly counseled *First thought, best thought!*—never rewrite.

And so, I'd never rewritten. Dashing off lines of poetry, outbursts of temper, regret, envy, spite, scorn, sarcasm, reproach, indignation. When I reread these lines afterward I saw that they were just—"emotions." I had not the patience or cunning to fashion such outbursts into actual poems: whatever art is, I could not achieve it.

Too bad, M. hadn't rendered these tender portraits into more permanent art. Perhaps she was afraid of seeming sentimental. Or not sentimental enough.

None of M.'s sculptures bore any resemblance to actual persons, the intimate impressions in the sketchbook would remain forever secret.

(Unless I reveal them. Eventually.)

Following these portraits of our parents were charcoal drawings of a fierce-faced young person with protuberant glaring eyes, the Fulmer jut-jaw, unkempt hair, an expression somewhere between anguish and rage: was this—*me*?

I stared and stared. For a weak moment, I thought I might faint.

How had M. seen the anguish in my soul? I'd kept it so disguised, I had thought.

The face wasn't ugly, though it was far from beautiful. Neither female nor male. The eyes were astonishing in their ferocity. There was no malice in the portrait, only a kind of sympathy, or pity on the part of the artist.

You see, M. loved you. For what you are.

Pulses beat hotly in my brain. I could not bear the prospect of another person seeing such a portrait of me, such an exposure.

If M. had rendered me ugly, as I am—if she'd rendered me spiteful, ironic, cruel, unfair, childish—that, perhaps

I could forgive. But not this: raw anguish, shading into terror.

Quickly I tore out the page, ripped it to shreds.

Wanting to destroy the entire sketchbook but no: it might be very valuable, one day.

If I am the executrix of M.'s estate, I will want to preserve such priceless documents.

If M. remained *missing*, there might be (posthumous) exhibits of her work. I intended to be prepared!

Whatever my personal feelings about the sketchbook.

Folded into the back of the sketchbook was a handwritten draft of a letter dated February 22, 1991, addressed to an administrator at the American Academy of Arts and Letters in New York City. Quickly I scanned it, only in rereading did I realize that it was a letter declining a prestigious award:

> Thank you for the great honor of the Prix de Rome. I wish that I could accept this generous offer of a fellowship year at the American Academy in Rome but, for family reasons, I believe that it is necessary for me to remain in Aurora for the time being.
>
> It may be that, sometime in the future, there will be a possibility that I might accept this fellowship, so I hope that you will keep my name

in mind. But if not, again thank you for this great
honor, which I regret I am not able to accept.

Family reasons. M. had declined this award for the sake
of Father and me!—without even telling us.

No doubt, she'd worried that something would happen
to me, if she left. Or to Father. Or both of us.

What that something might be, I have no idea.

Often I'd accused M. of wanting to leave Aurora,
returning to New York City and to her "glamorous" life
there. I'd laughed at her, I'd teased and tormented her,
for truly I was terrified by the possibility, just Father and
me alone in the house, where something terrible might
happen at any time. . . .

Coolly M. had insisted no, she had no plans to leave Aurora.
She was "very happy" and "very productive" in Aurora; she
was "very grateful" for her residency at the college.

*Remaining in Aurora to prevent something terrible from
happening to G.*

Instead, something terrible had happened to M.

◆

Now my eyes did spill tears. Now, hoarse sobs issued
from my throat.

33

"Portraits of Mortality." Troubling reports began to be told, how one of M.'s (male) artist-colleagues at Aurora College was "behaving strangely"—"suspiciously"—in the aftermath of her disappearance.

This "Elke"—(of course it had to be "Elke"!)—talked wildly and recklessly about M. to whoever would listen. He claimed to have "intimate information" about her—he claimed to be her "mentor." Soon he was behaving as if he were conducting his own, private investigation: daring to question, even to "grill," others at the college, about their relationships with M.; daring to approach, or try to approach, M.'s relatives in Aurora. (Of course, Father and I refused to see him.) It was noted that Elke seemed to be genuinely concerned that M. may have "met with foul play"—might be "imprisoned somewhere, against her will"—but his manner was aggressive and threatening and his questions rudely inappropriate as if he were, not a concerned colleague, but a jealous lover.

From what Father and I heard, thrillingly reported to us through gossipy relatives, Elke had tried immediately to attach himself to the police investigation, claiming that he had "intimate knowledge" of M.'s life; he'd made countless telephone calls to the police volunteering information that was already known to them, or of little consequence, or inaccurate. Elke boasted to Aurora detectives that while the Fulmer family would "hotly" deny it, he was closer to Marguerite than any of them. It was he, Elke, who was responsible for M. Fulmer being hired at the college. He'd been a "longtime confidante" of M.'s as well as her mentor.

Detectives soon became suspicious of Elke. Several times he turned up at police headquarters smelling strongly of alcohol. He spoke in outbursts, rambling monologues; then, abruptly, wondered aloud if he should "lawyer up" before he said more. He hinted at a "secret mission" of M.'s in which he had been a "trusted collaborator" but refused to elaborate further.

When detectives asked Elke bluntly if he and M. had had "relations" Elke said slyly: "Sir, that is a personal question. A gentleman keeps confidences."

Questioned about where he'd been on April 11 he asked another time if he should retain a lawyer—"Where is this headed?"

Elke was enormously pleased, it was said, when police took his fingerprints.

◆

"But are they letting that man *go*?"—Father protested. "Just letting him—*walk away*?"

I, too, thought it was odd: typically lackluster small-town police work. Though they had no evidence to link Elke with my sister's disappearance you'd think that Aurora police would wish at least to make it seem to the public as if they were *trying to find a suspect*.

◆

After my visit to M.'s studio, and our awkward meeting at the college, Elke seemed to assume that there was some sort of *rapport* between us. Hardly encouraged on my part!

Several times the flamboyant *artiste* dared to come to our house, and was turned away by Lena. He left notes which I read quickly, and tore to bits. He called, and left messages which were deleted (by me) without being heard. Once, he left a sumptuous bouquet on our front stoop—fragrant white lilies, white carnations, white roses loosely wrapped in tissue paper—with the scribbled note

In commiseration—our mutual loss—
your friend Elke

Of course, I thought that this bouquet was presumptuous, as well as ridiculous. I would have tossed it contemptuously into the trash except that Lena marveled at its beauty, and Father was quite beguiled by the scent of the lilies—(not knowing who'd left the flowers for us, for I had no intention of alarming him)—so despite my better judgment we kept the flowers, in a cut-glass vase, in the room we used most frequently, the kitchen.

Through the many rooms of our house, the scent of lilies—seductive, haunting . . .

Soon after this, the bewhiskered big-bellied *artiste* in the paint-splattered coveralls came into the Mill Street post office on the pretext of buying stamps!

My face flushed hot, seeing Elke in such close quarters: in the queue in front of my window, though the queue at the other window was shorter.

(At the Mill Street post office we see no reason to execute our duties swiftly. Initially it was I who set the pace, infuriating my co-workers with my methodical manner of waiting on customers; but soon then, they contrived a sort of undeclared contest with me, to see who can move most slowly, with a maddening attentiveness to details. Customers unfamiliar with our post office branch are perplexed at the slowness with which queues move; customers familiar with us, who live in the neighborhood, have grown accustomed to it, with a bemused sort of resignation. For we are *federal employees*, not easily terminated from our jobs.)

And so, one afternoon Elke appeared, looking earnestly at me, daring to smile inside his scruffy whiskers, as if I had not rebuffed him a dozen times! I had no choice but to wait on the man since I'd had a protracted restroom break just before this, and my co-workers would have protested loudly if I'd slipped away so soon again; but I resolved not to glance up at Elke, not to acknowledge him, and to ignore his absurdly mellifluous voice greeting me warmly, as if we were old friends.

After purchasing a sheet of stamps Elke asked me if he could meet me after the post office closed at 5 P.M. for a drink? coffee?

My cheeks were pounding with heat. Irritably I muttered: "I don't drink! I hate coffee!"

Still, my heart was pounding foolishly. The way Elke was regarding me, with a small sly smile, somewhat teasingly, not so swaggering or boorish now, was unexpected.

Halfway I feared that Elke would lurk about the post office, or just outside, waiting for me; but he did not.

That night in my room in my bed in the dark lying sleepless listening as the Aurora College bell tolled the early hours of the morning.

Why did M. reject Elke, was he not good enough for her? Was any man ever good enough for the Princess?

◆

By chance, on one of my long brooding walks, I decided impulsively to visit the Aurora public library (which I'd been boycotting for years since a contretemps with one of the smug spinster librarians whose name I will not mention) where several of Elke's portraits were hanging amid an exhibit titled, with grim unpromise, *Cayuga County Artists.*

Undeniably, Elke's canvases stood out from the usual pallid, simpering-pretty watercolors of sunsets, Cayuga Lake by moonlight, diminutive dimpled horses in snowy fields. Leapt to the eye like rude shouts.

Three paintings, quite large, of nude figures seated or reclining in dim-lit interiors: so far as I could determine—(I

163

did not want to be observed peering too closely at such sights)—the sex of the figures wasn't clear for the painter had caused their fleshy faces and bodies to melt even as backgrounds (wallpaper, a brick wall) were rendered with eerie precision. One of the figures appeared to be female—shapeless, like a great jellyfish verging upon the transparent. Wisps of dyed-red hair, eyes like floating fish. Pasty-pale dollops at which I did not wish to look too closely, fearing they would coalesce into breasts like udders. The title—*Muse.*

In black stylized letters, proudly positioned in the lower right-hand corner of each canvas, was *ELKE.*

My heart beat hard in opposition. Call this *art?*

I knew little and cared less about twentieth-century art—whether such experimental work had been influenced by Picasso, or Andy Warhol, or Walt Disney. I felt no ambiguity about Elke's paintings, however: they were discomforting, perverse.

Leaving the library quickly before the spinster-librarian saw me, that I might *breathe.*

And next day impulsively hiking to Aurora College where in the corridors of the arts school (as I'd recalled from my previous visit) there were works by faculty artists; and here too, several paintings by Elke similar to those in the library, big fleshy blatant nudes with melted-away faces and raw eyes, against fussy, elaborate backgrounds. Perverse, and repellent.

Yet, you did look. You could not help but *stare*.

None of the other faculty artists had created anything so eye-catching, if ungainly, as Elke. On a pedestal was one of M.'s signature vivid-white ovoids, about eighteen inches in height, resembling a disembodied and slightly deformed human head with smoothed-over surfaces where there might have been eyes, ears, nose, a mouth: *Soul 1*. I felt a small stab of loss, seeing it. One of M.'s more modest sculptures, more pitiable than pretentious now that its creator seemed to have vanished from the face of the earth.

Seeing that no one was in the corridor I stroked the head cautiously. I did not want to cause it to topple over, and shatter.

Expecting to feel only bland smoothness beneath my fingertips but feeling instead, with a shiver, something like tiny hieroglyphics etched into the stone, invisible to the eye.

She has left secret messages, has she? Left for the world to decipher after she has vanished.

If, that is, M. *had* vanished. For of course no one *vanishes*, as no one *goes missing*.

In a lounge nearby were more paintings by the ubiquitous Elke—"Portraits in Mortality." These were, if possible, more aggressively confrontational than the others hung in more public places: not blurred and impressionistic but shockingly realistic, human flesh and frailty in unsparing close-up.

All were reclining nudes, frontally presented. Not romantic-erotic flesh (*not* Renoir!) but stark *nakedness* of the kind rarely seen in classic art: skin textured with creases, blemishes, wrinkles, birthmarks, liver spots, rashes, striations, stretch marks, not smooth skin but doughy and pebbled. Skin that looked as if it had been fricasseed, left in the sun to bake. Skin loose, and skin tight to bursting as sausage casing. Again, the stark staring eyes that were pitiable, yet pitying.

D'you think you are not one of us? You are!

These were ugly, obscene. If I were a trustee of the college, I thought, I would demand that Elke's work be removed from public scrutiny.

(Of course, Father *was* a trustee. But I wouldn't have troubled him with such a petty request.)

Not even the (relatively) younger figures had been spared the cruelty of the relentless male gaze. Soft, shadowed flesh beneath eyes, grayish teeth, sagging frog-faces. Cone-shaped breasts, sunken chests, drooping bellies, swollen ankles. Except for flaccid breasts and wisps of pubic hair at groins you could barely identify the females;

the males, afflicted with glistening genital-sacs like goiters, were all too immediately identifiable.

Who were these people, who'd dared pose for Elke? They must have been friends or acquaintances: *Harvey, Millicent, Ella, Otto, Micah.*

Not professional models, obviously. But why on earth had anyone posed for Elke? How could anyone choose such self-punishment?

Still, the "Portraits in Mortality" were skillful, I supposed. Elke had a vision, however mean-spirited, and Elke had the technical skills to execute it. Such painstaking precision, up-close realism as if through a telescope, *I* could never do, I had to admit.

I wondered if, despite their differences, M. had admired Elke, grudgingly. She must have felt repugnance for the blustering male but, perhaps, not for his work. I knew that M. admired artists very different from herself—O'Keeffe, Hopper, Rothko, Picasso, and Matisse.

Standing very close to *Harvey*, I could almost see the sparse grizzly hairs on the man's fatty chest stir just perceptibly in my breath. The obscene shiny skin of drooping genitals, alarmingly realistic, uncomfortably close to my left hand . . .

"Hey! H'lo."

Startled I turned, to see Elke behind me, looking very pleased with himself.

"I thought that was you, Miss Fulmer—Georgia? Georgina? I thought I saw you in the corridor."

Deeply embarrassed, I wanted only to leave the exhibit. Escape!

At the same time thinking: *He has inquired after my name. He is interested in me.*

"The name is 'Georgene,' if you're interested." Coolly I spoke, though my face was feeling flushed.

"Ah, 'Georgene.' One of those rare feminizations of the masculine name that manage to sound more masculine than the original. 'George' is a trite little name, forgettable: 'Georgene' has gravitas."

Gravitas. I thought I knew what this meant. Not *heavy, ungainly* but significant, with dignity.

(Had to admit, I'd never thought of this before. My name had seemed appropriate to me, a sort of lumbering dinosaur, sexless and ungainly.)

(I *hated* it, that the name was a feminization of a male name. But it was for a woman I'd been named, evidently. Another insult.)

I wondered if Elke lay in wait, restless and distracted in his studio, to see if anyone apart from art students ambled along the hall; if anyone visited the exhibit in the (empty) lounge.

There was a certain excitement in Elke's face, a glittery sort of anticipation. My sensitive nostrils picked up just a hint of whisky on his breath.

"I'm flattered that you're interested in my work. There are some 'portraits in mortality' in private collections, you know, in Aurora and also in Ithaca. The state capitol museum has purchased a major canvas of mine and there's a sale pending to the Corning Museum. D'you have any questions about 'Portraits in Mortality'? I used a particular sort of brush for 'Harvey' to get that skin-texture—and the skin tone—I mix all my own colors, you know."

Elke was sounding eager, expansive, gregarious; here was the man's public self, that gloried in attention. No doubt attractive to a certain sort of culturally naive female.

But I was not one of these. I did not want to hear his bombast. I explained to Elke that I could not linger. I was expected home. In fact, I was late returning home.

Undeterred, Elke followed companionably beside me as I exited the lounge. He was a big man yet relatively quick on his feet like an upright bear. As if we were old friends he confided in me: how he'd been influenced by the British Lucian Freud's "unsparing eye," as well as by Francis Bacon. "We are a kind of triad, I believe. Art historians will note. In the mid-twentieth-century Freud and Bacon pioneered in a sort of nightmare hyper-realism of the body,

169

in the late twentieth-century Elke developed the vision to its aesthetic conclusion, and a little beyond."

Unblushing egotism!—*Freud, Bacon, Elke* in the same breath.

"I've been attacked by philistines just as Freud and Bacon were initially," Elke said, "—in fact, probably more since I chose to live in a provincial place. Several trustees of the college have complained: my work has been called 'corrupt'—'obscene'—'un-Christian.' But I have tenure, they don't dare try to fire me. It would be very bad publicity for Aurora College, which makes a pretense of admitting only the very best students when, it's known, one-third of admissions are legacies." Elke chuckled, considering.

Outdoors, I was conscious of Elke hovering close beside me, an overbearing figure in his paint-splattered coveralls, hair flowing in the wind like a TV Viking. On walkways undergraduate students glanced at us, curious, bemused. Two or three called out *H'lo Professor Elke!*—oblivious of how silly a name this was.

I could see how, the more time you spent in the man's presence, the less silly he seemed. There is a kind of erosion, a wearing away, in one's perception of foolishness, if the object of derision gives no sign that he acknowledges it.

With zest Elke stroked his whiskers as he spoke of the "bourgeois enemy"—"the perpetual adversary of the artist"—the "particular challenge of the nude."

"What the ordinary eye sees as ugly, the visionary artist transforms into beauty. Stand close to my portraits—(as, I saw, you were doing, Georgene)—and you become them. You are no longer the viewer—icy-calm, detached—as with M.'s sculptures. My art welcomes you *in*, you realize your common humanity—mortality."

"But—why?"

"'Why'—what?"

"Why would anyone want to realize anything 'common'—still less 'mortal'? *I* don't."

Nervously I laughed. Excitedly. The nearness of Elke was a goad, a dare. Like Elke I was feeling daring, reckless.

"Aha! You, too, like your sister, are fearful of the body—are you? Is this the female body you fear, or the male? Or—both?"

"Neither."

"Really! 'Neither.'"

In his deep-gravel voice Elke echoed my own voice. I heard a grudging approval, I thought.

No one had ever spoken to me quite like this. The barest suggestion that, in the estimation of someone of merit, G. might actually be more impressive than M.

171

Of course! You are Elke's type, outspoken and brazen. M. was too prim.

As if Elke could read my mind he said, with uncanny precision: "Yes. *You* are so much more down-to-earth than your sister. *She* imagined herself ethereal."

This was flattering! Badly I wished that M. could hear.

"You are a very different physical type, too. When you walk, you walk solidly on your heels. *She* moves like a ballerina."

Though Elke seemed to be speaking positively, I did not much like this comparison. Politely I told him that I had to leave now, I was awaited at home.

"Are you an *artiste*, Georgene? I think that you must be—an intransigent one."

Intransigent. I knew this word: a digging-in-the-heels word. Yes.

Carefully I explained: I was not an *artiste*. No one had coddled my pretensions as a child. No one had made excuses for me to pursue a selfish life. I'd had to be a "responsible" daughter to my mother when she was ill, and to my father who was devastated when my mother died; I could not focus upon my*self*, when I was needed elsewhere. Unlike my sister who'd thought nothing of going off to New York City and abandoning them.

Elke chuckled, amused. "Yes: *artistes* are selfish—self-hypnotized. Picasso said: 'Nothing interests me so much as the contents of my own mind.'"

As if you are Picasso! What a joke.

Politely I told Elke goodbye: my father was waiting for me at home.

(How likely was it that Milton Fulmer was waiting for his daughter at this time of day, when he was usually on the phone with his financial planner in New York City? But Elke, brash Elke, could have no idea.)

I walked away, flush-faced and panting. But smiling. Yes!

Elke did not pursue me. Gazing after me, I seemed to know, with a small fixed smile.

She, the sister. What is the name?—Georgene.

Descending the hill to Drumlin Road, that would bring me back, within a half hour, to the rear of our house on Cayuga Avenue, I heard the booming-braying male-elk voice call after: "I'll come to see you, Georgene! Soon."

34

A Visit from Detectives. Unknown to the *senior artist-in-residence* at Aurora College he'd been the object of police inquiries at our house that began soon after M.'s disappearance in April.

As Elke had (deliberately?) made himself suspicious to detectives they'd naturally asked Father and me about him: if he'd ever been a visitor to our house, so far as we knew; if he and my sister had "been on friendly or intimate terms" so far as we knew; and if M. had ever complained of Elke, or of anyone, having "stalked" her.

To these questions Father and I answered resoundingly: No, no, and *no.*

"You are certain?"—the plainclothes detective looked doubtfully at us, as if we might suddenly change our minds; as if we might suddenly recall an event we'd unaccountably forgotten.

For this is the (tedious) way of police inquiry: again, again, and again you are asked questions which you answer to the best of your ability; yet, you will be asked again, again, and again, and will have to practice patience, not to say snidely *Haven't you been listening? I've already answered that asinine question.*

However, the last time detectives asked me about Elke a malicious urge came over me, to tell them that I couldn't be sure that Marguerite *had not* mentioned Elke. I couldn't be sure that someone *was not* stalking M., and if that someone *was not* Elke.

Just this vague conjecture would be enough to get Elke into trouble. If he was now a "person of interest" in the investigation he might be reclassified as a "suspect."

Despite the publicity given to the investigation into M.'s disappearance, by several police departments of varying degrees of competence, not one genuine "suspect" had emerged by the end of the summer. They'd interviewed luckless saps like Walter Lang and other male friends, supposed lovers, acquaintances, and colleagues of my sister but had not arrested anyone for there was no evidence linking anyone to M.'s disappearance. There were no eyewitness accounts of any of these individuals interacting in any threatening way with M. There were no incriminating calls, letters.

And so, when I was asked, yet again, if "Elke" had ever visited our house, I hesitated just perceptibly before shaking my head *no*.

"You are sure, Ms. Fulmer? 'Elke' never visited your house?"

"To my knowledge, no."

"You're sure that your sister never invited him? Or—he'd come to see her?"

Again I hesitated. But then, shaking my head as if regretfully—*No*.

"And you'd never heard from anyone that 'Elke' might have been interested in your sister? Might have harassed her, followed her around? 'Stalked' her?"

No, and *no*.

Though in fact, as I wouldn't have confessed, if anyone had been harassing or stalking M. she would (probably) not have told Father and me. She'd never told me about the man who'd assaulted her when she'd been in high school; once or twice I'd tried shyly to bring up the subject and M. had glared at me, and turned away.

None of your business! I don't want your pity, or your sympathy.

Though I had no special reason to protect Elke, I did not want to cooperate with the investigation any more than might be expected of the distraught sister of the missing woman. I hate authority on principle: any kind of authority, usually male, that imagines it can tell me what to do. Law enforcement is of that type, like religion, and public health officials who insist that you must be vaccinated in line with their dictates. Petty tyrants! Weighing my proclivity for mischief against my proclivity to impede authority I decided to shake my head more emphatically *No*.

"My sister has too much taste than to be involved with anyone as crude as 'Elke.' That is all that I have to say on this vulgar subject."

Very carefully I'd said *has*, not *had*.

At this, the detectives exchanged glances. I felt my face flush with heat for I knew very well that they disliked me; for mediocre men always dislike assertive, fearless women. Yet, if the fools respected me, that was all I wished.

"One final question, Ms. Fulmer: has Elke approached *you*?"—this blindsided me, just a bit.

"Me! Why would . . ."

Now I was feeling truly distressed, irritated. For an awkward moment I could not speak at all.

"No, certainly not." Clearing my throat, to speak more clearly. *"He has not."*

Gravely they warned: "If Elke tries to approach you, let us know. He could be dangerous."

"'Dangerous'! *Him.*" Tried to laugh but I was shivering.

He has been a perfect gentleman with me, thank you.

There'd been "troubling things" reported to them about Elke, they said, notably his behavior with undergraduate women—"Nothing exactly actionable, but behavior that might be called threatening. A kind of sexual harassment, displaying his pictures of naked women. But he's smart enough to stay just this side of what he can get away with."

Pictures of naked women! What a simplistic description of "Portraits of Mortality."

I felt a sudden suffusion of hilarity, that these provincial plainclothes detectives, who knew nothing of me, of what I am capable, and how much I have borne, dared to imagine that I might be fearful of the swaggering bully-*artiste* Elke; or that they could presume, with the authority of their puerile brass badges, to advise *me.*

Enough! This interview was over.

Briskly I stood, to walk the detectives to the door. Again in ludicrous grave voices they warned me to avoid all contact with Elke and, if he tried to contact me, to call them immediately.

"Of course! I will do that—call you immediately. Thank you so much, Detectives! And Father thanks you too—you have been so helpful in finding my beloved lost sister, and bringing her back safely to us."

Shutting the door in the fools' startled faces, before they could react to my sarcasm carefully honed and glittering as a whetted razor.

35

"Tea-time." Yet, somehow it happened, on a brilliant autumn day when Father was out of town on business, and Lena had the afternoon off, and I'd called in sick at the post office, Elke came to visit at 188 Cayuga Avenue after all.

Just for "tea"—I'd insisted. Just for an hour.

So attentive had Elke been to me in recent weeks—(leaving little notes for me in our mailbox, dropping by the Mill Street post office to wait patiently in the line at my window, encountering me several times "by chance" on the street)—I'd finally laughed, and given in.

Very embarrassing! Especially when the bewhiskered hippie-haired *artiste* in the paint-splattered coveralls showed up at the post office to buy (yet another) sheet of stamps as my co-workers stared in amazement. *Is that person flirting with—Georgene Fulmer? How is that possible?*

My strategy has always been to ignore fools. And so, I ignored these ignorant busybodies.

Annoying at first, and then somewhat comical, and flattering, how Elke *persisted*. I was made to recall how, when Marguerite was in high school, one boy or another was always encountering her "by chance" after school—infatuated with my popular sister who ignored them, or laughed at them, or, from time to time, unpredictably, said *yes*, all right: she would go out with them.

For M. was unpredictable. Perhaps all beauty is *unpredictable* which is why the impulse to destroy it is so strong.

But this was the first time that a man had followed me. The first time in my life I'd encountered masculine *persistence*.

Elke had wanted to take me for lunch or dinner at the historic Aurora Inn: the first such invitation of my life which (ah, I had no choice!) I'd had to decline, reluctantly; for news of such a brazen public outing would get back to Father immediately, and Father would be furious at his daughter's (seeming) consorting with a (seeming) notorious local "suspect."

No way to explain to Father that Elke, for all his swaggering machismo, was (in fact) a gentleman, and respectful of me; that, indeed, Elke recognized a kinship between us, that had not existed between him and Marguerite. No way to explain to Father who was hyper-vigilant and suspicious of virtually everyone in Aurora, and ever more convinced that half the people he encountered knew more than they were admitting about M.'s disappearance, that Elke was, surely, *not dangerous*: not a threat.

"If not a meal at the Aurora Inn, Georgene, then—maybe—a walk along the lake shore? A drive around the lake?"—so Elke pleaded. "This beautiful autumn weather won't last forever, you know. Soon it will be winter and only the most adventurous will emerge out of their burrows."

Gaily Elke spoke, like a man who has been drinking: festive, exhilarated, a little reckless. I did feel a slight frisson of alarm for this (odd) talk of burrows had a dark edge to it.

He wants me to think that he knows where M. is. Where she is buried—in a burrow . . .

Nervously I laughed, short of breath. Elke's glittery-reptilian eyes on me were disconcerting but exciting.

"We have so much to say to each other, Georgene. After all."

This, uttered with an air of jocular reproach, as if I were denying something perfectly evident.

It was true, Elke and I talked together with surprising ease, intimacy. It had begun in M.'s studio at the college—our first exchange. Of course we had the subject of M. to discuss but much more than merely M; indeed, M. was turning out to be but the starting point of our relationship.

Though I was tempted to go for a drive with Elke around the lake, this also might be too public an excursion, and might be reported back to Father. (Indeed, it might have been reported back to the busybody detectives!) Instead, impulsively I invited Elke to come for tea at my house, for just an hour—"While Father, and our housekeeper, are away. We can be very private."

"'Private'! Yes, good." Elke beamed with anticipation.

My face pounded with heat. Oh, I had not meant to say what I'd said—*private* was not the word I'd meant.

"The first 'tea-time' of my life," Elke said, with a wink.

So, on a balmy October day Elke arrived at our house promptly at 4:30 P.M. I had been waiting anxiously since at least 3 P.M.

In fear that Elke would not show up, and in fear that Elke *would* show up.

The first surprise: Elke was wearing, not his usual paint-splattered coveralls, but denim jeans and jacket, that fitted his rotund figure somewhat tightly; around his

183

neck on a leather thong was a Native American–looking carved wooden owl. His mood was jaunty and his wavy, shoulder-length graying hair and whiskers gleamed with a synthetic luster.

Greeted, by me, with some nervous awkwardness, Elke stepped into the foyer of our house staring and blinking, clearly intimidated by the size of the house, and perhaps by its grimly regal English Tudor design; but, in his role as *artiste*, rebel, and super-macho male, stalwart adversary of the bourgeoisie, he couldn't resist making sardonic comments of a joshing nature: "Well! Ms. Georgene Fulmer!—you and your sister managed to get born into a *très comfortable* lifestyle, yes?"

I winced just a bit, at this immediate allusion to M., but managed to laugh good-naturedly.

Saying, in the pert tart tone of a spirited young woman in a romantic comedy, "You are correct: we 'got born' into it. Just accident, like 'not being born' into it."

This seemed, to me, a witty rejoinder. But Elke responded with a cavalier shrug of his shoulders.

"No need to apologize, Georgene. I myself was born into 'comfort'—American upper-middle-class pretensions—upon which I turned my back at the age of eighteen."

Boldly, uninvited, Elke strode past me to peer into the living room, whistling thinly through his teeth. "What

184

are these, antiques? Carved mahogany? 'Oriental' carpet?
Looks like a museum."

"Well. We rarely use the room . . ."

"Of course you don't. Smells of embalming fluid."

The man's rudeness seemed totally unpremeditated: I
stood staring after him like one who has unwisely opened
a door, and has no idea how to close it again. Was this the
first time in my life that I'd invited a friend into my father's
house? A *man friend*?

Too late, Georgene. You can only make a fool of yourself.

. . . an endangered fool, indeed.

Though I'd made no move to show Elke the interior of
the house, or to switch on lights in these dimly lighted
downstairs rooms, Elke continued to the next room, which
Mother had called the drawing room, glancing curiously
about at framed paintings on the walls, the thick Chinese
carpet, velvet-cushioned sofas and chairs, the Steinway
spinet. "Jesus! What a beautiful piano. Is it real?" Roughly
he opened the keyboard that hadn't been opened in years;
struck a note, and another, stridently. "Out of tune."

Bit my lip not to stammer some foolish apology. What is
this power of bullies, that, though brazen and rude, they
make the rest of us feel insecure, inclined to apologize for
disappointing them? And why should I care, if M.'s piano
is out of tune?

"D'you play piano, Georgene?"

Georgene. My name on Elke's lips had a strange effect upon me: weakness, tremor, excited anticipation, a desire to laugh wildly.

Even as I was thinking *Yes but the man is manipulating you. He has gained entrance to the house where his presence is forbidden. Take care!*

Embarrassed as an adolescent girl I murmured not so much, any longer.

"Did M. play piano?"—I'd steeled myself for this seeming-casual query.

"Not really. She gave up soon, I persevered years longer."

So readily did these (harmless) fibs leap from my tongue, so easily Elke seemed to believe them, I was feeling elated as a balloon filling with helium.

So easy, I thought. Elke and I are so easy together.

"Hmm. What's this?"—Elke had noticed a landscape painting on a wall, inside a particularly heavy, gilt frame. He leaned close, squinting. "This is a Blakelock? *Really?*"

A dark-hued heavy-clouded landscape of no evident distinction with tall spreading elms, enshadowed, over-looking a small lake. The painting itself was not large; the gilt frame dwarfed it. Why anyone would take the trouble to paint such a bland country scene was a mystery to me: I'd been seeing the painting, and not-seeing it, all my life.

Not wanting to seem ignorant I told Elke guardedly that I thought so, yes—"'Blacklock.' It's been here forever."

"*Blakelock*. Ralph Albert Blakelock. American artist, 'gothic,' nineteenth century. This is obviously a minor work but still, quite valuable."

Quite valuable. I had no idea what this might mean: five hundred dollars, five hundred thousand dollars? In a secondhand store the painting wouldn't have been worth more than twenty-five dollars, I was sure.

On the wallpapered drawing room walls were several ornately framed oil paintings that no one had looked at seriously, before Elke, within my memory. Like most of the furnishings of the house these had been inherited from Fulmer grandparents who'd been born long ago, in the nineteenth century, when there were no taxes—no federal or state taxes, no income taxes, no property taxes. Our "robber baron" ancestors, M. used to call them with a little sniff of disdain.

Of course, Marguerite Fulmer had enjoyed the privileges of being a *Fulmer*, even as she disdained them.

"Jesus! Is this a *Ryder*?"

Elke was peering excitedly at a small oil painting: a seascape, but very dark, luminous, blurred as if seen through a scrim. In the sky, a dull-glowering little moon, reflected brokenly in waves thick as molasses. This (weird) painting too, I'd been seeing, and not-seeing, all my life but I had no idea who the artist was: *Ryder?*

"It is! 'Albert Pinkham Ryder'—'Moonrise.' But the surface is badly deteriorated—it's cracking. He painted with bitumen which turns black with time. Plus the air is too dry in this house—you need some sort of climate control for art as fragile as this." Elke laughed, as if exasperated by my look blank as a Kleenex. "Doesn't anyone in your family care? Doesn't anyone *know*? Surely M. realized that this is a rare Ryder . . ."

More of M.! Oh why were we always talking of *M*.!

Stiffly I said that, as I recalled, M. hadn't taken any more notice of the "art" in our house than I had.

(Was this true? M. had felt estranged from the "robber barons"—that was it.)

Like a professor confronting a particularly dull-witted student Elke explained: Albert Pinkham Ryder had been an eccentric nineteenth-century American artist who'd lived into the twentieth century but had always been an outsider. Solitary, unworldly, unprofessional as an artist not concerned with the preservation of his work, a creator of a kind of private iconography—"poetic"—"mystical."

He'd had a long career as an artist but there weren't many of his paintings in existence; and of these, quite a few were damaged beyond repair.

As if the idea had just come into his head Elke said he'd take the painting to a "restorer." He knew someone in Syracuse.

"These tiny cracks in the surface—see? If it isn't treated the paint is going to chip off. But it isn't too late—maybe."

Elke made a move to take the painting down from the wall. Suddenly I was wary, alarmed.

No! Father would miss the painting, I protested. It would be too difficult to explain to him where it was . . .

Seeing that Father knows who you are, and loathes you. Considers you a "suspect" in M.'s disappearance.

Quickly Elke said: "Look—I'll give you a substitute. I can easily make a simulacrum, just this size. I can find a frame in a secondhand shop. I know just the paints I'd use: viridian, iridescent white, cobalt blue, but mostly midnight-black. I mix my own paints! I could do it in an hour. The painting is almost too dark to make out details, as it is. Easiest thing in the world to copy. Dull moon, moonlight on the water. Everything smudged. Blurred. Dreamlike. Typical Ryder: kitsch, but authentic kitsch, not cheesy. Of course, I can't reproduce the tiny cracks but your father won't notice, I guarantee."

189

Hypnotized I listened to Elke's plotting. Amazing to me, Elke knew so much about this art of another era, totally unlike his own. And he seemed truly to *care*.

Then, a voice of common sense admonished me. *No. Impossible.*

"Please—no. I—I can't let you take the painting away. Not just now."

Weakly I spoke, apologetically. It seemed that I was more afraid of my father's wrath than of Elke's disappointment.

"What do you mean, 'not just now'? Some other time, then? Why?"

Elke was frowning. His fingers twitched, he so much wanted to remove the little painting from the wall and bear it away with him.

I stammered: Father would see immediately that the painting was missing. He was very attached to the antique things in the house. . . .

"Of course: the Ryder on the wall. He'd notice. The man takes great interest in his collection—obviously." Sarcasm heavy as lead, as if Elke were stepping on my foot harder, harder, and harder.

I promised Elke that I could bring up the subject of the Ryder painting to Father, soon. I would ask him to examine it, and see how the surface was cracking; I would then suggest that someone from the art school come to examine it, to provide professional advice . . .

"And that someone would be—me? Or—?"

"That—that 'someone' would be *you*."

"And then—?"

"And then—what?"

"Your father would have the painting restored? He'd spend that much money, on a painting no one ever looks at?"

"If it's famous as you say it is . . ."

"Well, not *famous*. But rare."

It came over me, Elke wanted to appropriate the painting. His plan was theft.

He would take away the painting, and leave us a "simulacrum" in its place. And I would never dare reveal the theft to Father, out of cowardice.

Deftly, with a broad smile, Elke changed the subject: "The hell with 'Moonrise.' Let's have—'tea.'"

This was a relief. I was eager to escape the older, darker part of the house which seemed to be provoking tension between my visitor and me.

With pride I led Elke into a sunroom at the rear of the house, overlooking Cayuga Lake. Here, everything was lighter, airier, less cluttered with "antiques"; no wall hangings because the walls were all plate glass. A floor of russet-red Spanish tiles which M. had chosen.

"Beautiful!"—Elke exclaimed, without irony.

Now, he will like me again. Now it will be all right.

Hurriedly I excused myself, to fetch the tea things.

First time in my entire life: *serving tea.*

In the kitchen breathless I reheated the water in the kettle, to a boil, then poured the water into the teapot, to let the Earl Grey tea(bags) steep. I am not at ease in a kitchen, which, I tend to think, is a "woman's place"—(I do not identify with "woman" if I can help it: "woman" is likely to be a sap); preparing tea for Elke was a profound occasion, requiring calculating, following instructions on the box of tea. I'd had the presence of mind to rinse out dusty Wedgwood teacups untouched for years; I hoped that Elke, for all his bluster about *très comfortable* lives, would appreciate their fragile, costly beauty.

When I brought teapot, cups, sugar and cream and Scottish oatmeal "biscuits" on a tray into the sunroom, Elke stared with a blank look like a disappointed baby. "You were serious about 'tea'—I guess."

"Oh, would you prefer coffee?"—I was stricken with embarrassment, for having made another blunder.

"D'you have a beer? Wine?"

"Father has Scotch whisky . . ."

"Well. Don't go out of your way." Elke spoke neutrally but with an obvious air of hope.

192

The rough-textured oatmeal biscuits were favorites of my father's, which came in a colorful red-plaid tin from Edinburgh; expensive, but not very tasty (I thought), possibly a little stale but Elke bit into one and chewed hungrily.

Cayuga Lake was becoming agitated. A wind was rising fretfully at the end of the day. Earlier, there'd been sunshine; now the sky was eclipsed by hammerhead clouds. I calculated that we had at least ninety minutes before Father returned; and if Lena returned sooner it would not greatly matter, for Lena would never tell Father anything to disturb him. Never would Lena have whispered to her employer—*Your daughter has brought a dangerous "suspect" into the house in your absence.*

Hurriedly I went to fetch a bottle of Father's from his cabinet of whiskies—*Macallan Highland Single Malt Scotch Whisky.* It had been opened and was three-quarters full.

As Elke looked on approvingly I poured the warmly brown liquid into a whisky glass. I wondered if I was supposed to add something else—water, ice cubes? But Elke took the glass gratefully from my fingers, swallowed, nodded. "Yes. This will do. Thank *you.*"

Soon then, as we talked together, Elke took the bottle to set beside his glass. "I can serve myself, Georgene. No need for you to wait on me."

193

As it was rare for me to entertain a visitor, I searched my thoughts for something to say that *was not* related to my missing sister; but Elke sighed heavily, and smiled sadly, and said, as if he'd just now thought of it: "D'you think, Georgene, that you could show me Marguerite's room? I promise, I wouldn't touch a thing."

"I—don't think so. I'm sorry."

Stiffly I spoke. Sipping at Earl Grey tea that had steeped too long, and was brackish-vile on the tongue. Elke saw the expression on my face, of acute annoyance, and hurt; and nodded in sympathy, fixing me with widened, slightly bloodshot eyes.

"M.'s room is upstairs," I said carefully. "Rooms—she had a kind of apartment. *Has* a kind of apartment. It has been left undisturbed—mostly. Father is certain that M. will return."

"But police searched the rooms, yes?"

"Y-Yes. Police did search the rooms." In fact, several teams of police officers, at several times. *Hateful*. "But we were present, Father and me; and we didn't let them tear it apart. And now—it's as it had been, or mostly."

"On the second floor, did you say? Where, exactly?"

"This side of the house, with a view of the lake."

"Very nice. But not surprising."

Between us, that *frisson* of rapport, Elke and me, in opposition to M.

Apologetically I said: "I just don't think—I mean, Father wouldn't think it would be appropriate for a stranger to be shown Marguerite's quarters. . . ."

"Would 'Father' have to know about it, Georgene?" Elke all but winked at me, teasing.

"I—I—I would be concerned he would find out."

"But how would 'Father' find out, if you didn't tell him?"

"He might—somehow—know . . ."

This was so weakly uttered, Elke took mercy on me. "I understand, Georgene. Of course. Though, you know, I am not a stranger to Marguerite. You know that."

Were you her lover? And do you love her, still?

I was quiet. I felt rebuked. My heart churned in my chest, in clumsy distress.

Elke turned the conversation to a general topic: contemporary art, its excesses and aspirations. How the "vacuous beauty" of Abstract Expressionism yielded to the "randy nose-thumbing" of Pop Art; how Pop Art made possible a "revolutionary return" to figurative art, given a great boost by the "late, savage" work of Philip Guston, one of Elke's heroes. And now, more recently, the bold brazen unflinching nudes of Lucian Freud . . . Through a buzzing in my ears I listened, or half listened, as, as if inevitably, by this circuitous route Elke returned to the subject of M: the

195

"radical differences" between his art and hers yet, para-
doxically, their "mutual respect" for one another—their
"intimate rapport."

I resented M. always present in this house!—when in
fact M. was *absent*.

And was any of this true?—I wondered. Did Elke actually care for my sister, or was Elke morbidly obsessed
with her; was the self-aggrandizing *artiste* capable of love,
whatever love was, a puzzlement to me, or was he merely
infatuated? Or—merely *pretending*?

For often I wonder: is love mostly *pretense*?

Elke asked if I had any photographs of M. that I might
show him, family pictures, whatever—"I'd so appreciate
it, Georgene."

As it happened I'd been looking through family albums
over the summer. Going through Mother's albums of Marguerite and me as children. It was somewhat deflating,
that Mother had lavished such care upon her firstborn
daughter, of whom there were, I am not exaggerating,
hundreds of snapshots; when I was born, six years after
Marguerite, much of the zest had gone out of motherhood,
it seemed, for there were far fewer of little Georgene (ridiculous name!) in *her* cradle, or swaddled in *her* (smiling)
mother's arms. Unmistakably, to be *second-born* is to be
second-rate.

For most of M.'s childhood, M.'s photographs were neatly positioned in the albums; with the passage of time, Mother lost interest in such caretaking, and photographs, snapshots, memorabilia were loose amid the albums' pages, including (of course) most of anything pertaining to me. Many (very flattering) photos of Marguerite as a young girl, an adolescent, an older teenager; (not so flattering) photos of Georgene, all but lost among M.'s, spilling out of the albums when they were carelessly lifted.

Why I gave in to Elke's request, I am not sure. Perhaps I feared that he would grow bored soon, finish a second, or a third, drink, and leave; and I would feel wounded in his wake, that he'd been in the house, in the sunroom, in *my presence,* and had slipped away like a fish slipping free of a hook in his mouth.

(Though I had not a clue what one did, with a hooked fish. *With an adult man?*)

Elke stared at the photographs, enraptured. Sipping Father's Scotch whisky.

The earliest baby pictures of Marguerite, and pictures of Marguerite as a toddler, blond, blond hair in ringlets, dimpled cheeks, heartbreaking beauty, sometimes just perceptibly *pouting, sulking*—though usually a sweet smile; in her wake, like a rowboat in the wake of a yacht, came the younger sister Georgene, not an ugly child, nor even a homely child, perhaps one might say a *plain-faced child* with an unfortunate jawline; not-blond hair, and not-blond-ringlets; at a disadvantage when sharing a picture with the older sister, a mistake she'd learned to avoid when a little older.

As we turned the pages of the second album, dazzled by the nascent blond beauty of the elder girl, setting into cruel relief the less-than-beauty of the younger, wanting to hide my eyes with my spread fingers as I'd done as a child. Marguerite as a girl in middle school, in high school, departing for college; poor clueless clunky Georgene as a girl of ten, eleven, twelve who'd smiled too hard for the camera, like a Hallowe'en pumpkin, or refused to smile at all, glaring-eyed, forehead-furrowed, jut-jawed . . . Quick leap to high school, abruptly stork-tall, spindly limbed, blemished skin, frowning in graduation powder-blue gown and matching cap with a tassel foolishly dangling over her forehead.

"This is a very attractive picture of you, Georgene. You are an attractive woman."

So earnestly did Elke utter these words, so (seemingly) without guile, I burst into laughter. But still, my face smarted with blood in a rush.

Fool, fool! Was I falling in love? With the swaggering boorish *artiste* whom M. had rejected?

◆

He had a theory, Elke said, about M.'s *whereabouts.*

Had to stifle laughter, that word *whereabouts.* Such a cliché!

On the lake, waning ripples of light. Dusk comes early in October, in upstate New York.

Elke's words were beginning to slur. His large face glowed, whisky was warming him to his subject: "In the matter of a 'disappearance,' there are usually two theories: the missing person has been abducted, or the missing person has left of her own volition, in secret. But there's a third possibility: the 'missing person' has never left but is buried in her hometown. Murdered, buried. In Aurora."

"Really!"—my tea had gone stone-cold.

"There was that 'psychic'—'astrologer'—remember? The woman was interviewed in the paper. Claiming that Marguerite was 'in hiding' in Aurora . . . Not sure what happened to her, there hasn't been anything about her in months."

Again I said, "Really!"

"Of course, astrology is just bullshit. 'Psychics'— I suppose some people have a kind of 'second sight,' intuition—hunches. D'you know what happened to her? 'Mildred Pierce.'"

If this was a trick to entice me, I did not succumb to it. So far as I was concerned, Mildred Pierce was as good as Mildred Pfeiffer.

Neatly if shallowly disposed of. Hard-packed dirt, rendered odorless.

Tap-tap-tapping with the flat of the shovel. Good work!

"Of course, there are some who think that M. committed suicide, in the lake. Drowned herself." Elke hesitated, a pained look in his face. "Not near here—somewhere else. The lake is too large—too deep—to be dredged."

A pause. Elke swallowed more whisky as if to comfort himself.

"Did M. share with you, Georgene, secrets of her 'private life'? She'd hinted of men—lovers—kept unaware of one another . . ."

To this, I shook my head in silence. Meaning to signal ambiguity: maybe *yes,* maybe *no.*

". . . unaware of each other. We were."

A flush had come into Elke's heavy face. A look of anguish and vexation.

Saying: "But M. wasn't the 'type' for suicide. Absolutely not! She lived for her work, and her work enthralled her. She had an exhibit scheduled for January, in Chelsea.

She'd won an award from the American Academy, a year's residency in Rome, did you know?"

"Did she! I'm not sure if we knew."

Why M. hadn't told Father and me. A mystery, which I resented.

"She'd told our departmental chair, and me, of course—but no one else. There was some problem about her accepting the residency in Rome, I think she'd wanted to defer it. Or, she'd felt that she had to defer it. I told her for Christ's sake take it, not to hesitate! I'd come to visit her in Rome, I said. Proud as hell of her, she was my protégé."

"Yes, you've said. Several times."

"She spoke of me to you, didn't she? As her 'mentor'?"

"I'm not sure . . ."

"Her mentor, her friend, and her colleague. Surely she *did*."

"Well—yes. I think—yes, she did."

This was not remotely true. M. had rarely discussed her colleagues at Aurora, with me at least; and never Elke, I was sure. Never a *man*.

I did not want to contradict Elke, he would have liked me less. I was alarmed to feel his interest in me sliding away, like a marble on a tilted tabletop. If I adjusted the table just right, the marble would cease rolling away.

201

It seems that, without realizing it, I'd poured some of the Macallan whisky into my teacup and had been tasting it, with my tongue. Such a sensation!

In a lowered voice, as if he thought someone might overhear, Elke brought up the subject again of M.'s quarters: "I would really like to see them, Georgene. Where she slept. Just for a moment. You'd said the police have searched the rooms. I wouldn't touch anything."

I hesitated. Where was the harm? Elke would be grateful, his gratitude would spill onto me like sunshine. But something kept me from agreeing.

"You've been so generous sharing these photographs with me. I much appreciate it. And you see, nothing has been damaged or out of place. If I could just peek into her bedroom . . ."

"M-Maybe another time. It's getting late, Father will be home soon."

Another time. Another visit. Come back. Yes!

Elke cast me a sidelong look of sheer hatred which, a moment later, had vanished, so swiftly that I could doubt I'd seen it.

Now, disappointed but smiling, determined to be a good sport: "Well. You've been very kind, Georgene. You love your sister very much, I can see, and want to protect her privacy. As I do, also—of course."

Elke made a movement to rise to his feet, inadvertently knocking one of the albums onto the floor. A dozen snapshots fell out, scattering; we bent over, to pick them up.

"Your sister was—*is*—a beautiful woman," Elke said, sighing, as he examined one of her photographs, "—but beauty can be exasperating, it's so smug."

I laughed. Yes! I'd often thought this.

"Beauty seems so self-sufficient. Not like us."

Us. Was this flattery, or not? Insult? I wasn't sure.

The Wedgwood teacup quivered in my hand: empty. Neither Earl Grey tea nor whisky remained.

The sensation in my tongue had expanded to the entire inside of my mouth, and my throat. A silly smile forced my lips apart.

"I would like very much to meet your father, Georgene. If not today, next time."

To ask for your hand in marriage. The thought came to me with such wild abandon, I had to laugh.

"Is something funny, dear?" Elke smiled, a bit coldly.

Dear. This, too, was funny.

A man does not want to be laughed *at* but laughed *with*. By instinct, I knew this, and so quickly amended:

"No! Not at all. Not funny—at all. It's a wonderful idea, to meet Father sometime, to come for a family dinner here.

Our housekeeper Lena is an excellent cook, I help her in the kitchen, we have our favorite recipes. Especially if it's explained to Father that you were Marguerite's mentor, Father would be grateful, I'm sure."

Eagerly I spoke. A warm flame-y sensation in my throat, in my upper chest, in the region of my heart.

But now I was beginning to worry: my visitor should leave, before Father returned.

Father's car would turn into the driveway, he would drive to the rear of the house and park in the garage, beside M.'s Volvo, untouched since April. By the time I heard the car door slam shut in the garage, if I heard it—it would be too late . . .

"Excuse me, Georgene—may I use a bathroom? I'll be just a minute."

Rising to his feet, swaying. The reptile-eyes were bright, glittering. Oh, why hadn't I urged Elke to leave, ten minutes before! The whisky had gone to my head, I wasn't thinking clearly.

No choice but to lead Elke to one of the downstairs guest bathrooms, near the kitchen. Disconcerting, how the man swayed on his feet with a kind of cheerful obliviousness, like a large drunken child. I hurried to stand in the foyer, to watch nervously for Father's car.

Steadily, the sky darkened. Streetlights came on, in the distance. Headlights appeared, ascending Cayuga Avenue. I held my breath: the headlights turned in another direction.

It seemed to me that Elke was taking an unconscionably long time. Had he fallen asleep in the bathroom! Would I be able to waken him! A vision came to me, of Lena and me, struggling to wake the big-bellied *artiste* and walk him out of the house before Father arrived.

Another pair of headlights on Cayuga Avenue, headed in this direction. And again, at the last possible moment, turning away . . .

Trying not to become desperate. Frantic. Wondering if Elke had left the bathroom by now and was wandering through the house. Possibly, he'd become lost. I did not want to think that I was hearing footsteps on the stairs—footsteps overhead. Stealthy footsteps. *He is looking for M.'s room in defiance of me.*

"I won't hear. I don't hear."

Pressing the (sweaty) palms of my hands over my ears.

Elke couldn't know: the door to M.'s room was locked in any case. The key was hidden in Father's bedroom. Someone might break into our house in the night and search through M.'s room, and we wouldn't know.

205

He will be so surprised! Turning a doorknob, and the door doesn't open.

I had not noticed headlights but suddenly I heard, or believed that I heard, the sound of a car motor at the rear of the house, shutting off. The rattling sound of the garage door being lowered. My heart beat rapidly, at the risk I was taking. Did I hear?—was I hearing—something?

I ran into the hall. I called for Elke, who appeared abruptly, looking harried. The flush in his face had deepened, the reptilian eyes had dimmed slightly. If he'd been upstairs, and had been disappointed, he was too clever to give a sign.

But now, Father was home, unmistakably. I heard a car door slam just barely in the garage, for the blood beating in my ears. Tugging at Elke's arm, to urge him to the front door. "I'm sorry—you must leave."

"Must I!"—Elke laughed, staggering clumsily against me like an upright bear.

"My father is home . . ."

"Is he!"

Elke was laughing at me, at my distress, but took pity on me now, seeing my anxious face, my gnarled frightened soul, so rarely exposed, it must have gleamed pinkly, like an obscene inner organ from which you quickly looked away.

At the front door Elke groped for my hand, squeezing hard enough to make me wince.

"Thank you, dear Georgene! May I come again to you, soon? I will call you."

Astonishingly, Elke lifted my hand to kiss my knuckles, wetly.

Faint-headed, I shut the door firmly behind Elke. Even as Father entered the house into the kitchen calling in a pettish voice: "Lena! Georgene! Why aren't the lights on back here?"

36

The Suitor. Phone rang, Lena answered. Called (warily) upstairs to me: "For you, Georgene."

Because no, I don't run to the phone. *Do not breathlessly run to the damned phone like a hyperventilating thirteen-year-old* though yes, I'd been waiting for his call.

His. No need to name.

And yes, "warily": Lena was respectful of my moods, which tended, even from my own perspective, to be unpredictable.

Still, heart pounding in the very palm of my hand as I picked up the receiver, for each time the phone rang it might be *him* as each toss of the dice might be the winning toss and so each risk taken was worth it and should not be regretted.

But it was Denise. High-pitched, incredulous.

"Georgene! I've been hearing the most surprising—shocking—things about you: you have a *suitor*, who has come to your *house*!"

"A—what?"

"A 'suitor.'"

"Suit-er? What—what is that?"

My mind had gone blank. Blinding light in conjunction with deafening noise was sweeping over me.

"*'Suit-or'*—a man who comes to call on a woman, with the hope of proposing marriage."

Denise spoke with bemused irony, as one might speak to a slow-witted child.

Now I began to comprehend. An immense wave of heat washed over me, as if a furnace door had been flung wide open before my stunned eyes.

Just two days after Elke's visit. Which, I was sure, no one knew about—*no one*.

For Father hadn't known, and Lena hadn't known. *No one had known about the visit except Elke.*

Since that visit had come to an abrupt end I'd been thinking of little else. *May I come again to you, soon? I will call you.*

And so, I'd been expecting a call. At any time. Eager to check messages when I returned home from the post office.

Lifted the receiver with eager timidity even when there'd been no (evident) call, no ringing of the phone. As if (somehow) there might be a message which I had missed.

"Who told you this, Denise? Who's been gossiping about me?"

"Well—is it true?"

"I said—*who* has been gossiping about me?"

Denise had a maddening habit, simply ignoring questions she didn't wish to answer. Yet more maddening, my cousin's pretense of incredulity as if the mere possibility that a man might visit me, whether a "suitor" or otherwise, was so ludicrous.

"This—'artist in residence' at the college—supposedly a colleague of M.'s—how on earth did you meet him? What is going on, Georgene?"

Somehow, Denise knew about Elke. Aurora is a small town, everyone knows too much about everyone else, but I'd thought—(I'd thought!)—that that did not include *me*.

It made me furious, to think that people were talking about me. No doubt, Fulmer relatives who lived on Cayuga Avenue, who must have noticed an unfamiliar car parked in front of our house . . . Busybodies who'd always gossiped about Marguerite, because they were jealous of her, and about me, because I was—well, what *was* I?

Gigi has a suitor, who has come to her house!

I laughed. Feeling both embarrassment and a little flame-flicker of pride.

Calmly I heard myself say: "His name is 'Elke.' He isn't just a college instructor, he's a nationally known artist—Marguerite's 'mentor.' And I didn't meet him, he met *me*. When I went to M.'s studio, back in April, Elke introduced himself to me, and offered any help he could give us."

Us was judiciously chosen. *Us* included not only Father, but all the Fulmers.

"They were friends, apparently. They collaborated on art projects together though they had 'antithetical' views of art."

I could imagine Denise's face. *Antithetical views of art.* No idea what on earth this might mean.

"Georgene! Do you mean that you'd *invited him*? It was—*deliberate*?"

"Yes. Elke came to see me, by invitation. For tea. The man is a gentleman, he wouldn't have come uninvited."

"What kind of a name is 'Elke'? Is that—a kind of moose? That can't be the man's real name."

"I wouldn't know about that," I said coldly. "His name is his own business."

"Georgene, was your father present, at this 'tea'?"

"No. Father was working."

211

"Well: does your father *know*?"

At this, I was silent. Denise was treading very close to dangerous territory here. She knew, and I knew that she knew, that she must not hint to me that she might tell Father, who was her uncle, her father's older brother. That would be unforgiveable.

"Father does not know—yet. But Elke will be returning, he's impressed with the art in our house, and has plans for its restoration. He will be meeting soon with Father to discuss this."

"Art? What art in your house?"

"You wouldn't recognize the names, Denise. 'Blackmore,' 'Ryder.' Nineteenth-century American artists."

"Those old paintings on your walls? Those are actual *art*?"

Denise was sounding so incredulous, I bit my lower lip to keep from saying something rude.

"What I've been hearing is—this man is interested in *you*? He's *courting* you?"

Courting! Had to laugh, I'd never heard such a preposterous thing.

Denise was treading very close to insult, in the way she continued to speak to me. As if I, her cousin Georgene, could not have reasonably interested, attracted a man.

Recalling years ago, when we were girls. How I'd leapt at Denise, a cousin, to strangle her, for teasing and tormenting me. Marguerite had pulled me off Denise but not before I'd frightened both of them.

Except: had that been Denise, or a younger sister of hers? Maybe the younger sister.

"Elke and I are 'soul mates'—he has said. We'd bonded over our concern for Marguerite but as it turns out, we're far more like each other than either of us is like Marguerite."

There, I'd stated it clearly. The bond. The mysterious connection.

"Georgene, what on earth does that mean—'soul mate'?"

"If you don't know, it can't be explained to you. I have to hang up now."

"No, wait! Georgene! Don't you realize, this 'Elke' is dangerous? People say he's a 'suspect' in whatever happened to Marguerite—he might be arrested any day. Don't you realize that this person who is 'courting' you might be responsible for—for what happened to Marguerite?" Denise was breathing hard. She didn't say *responsible for Marguerite's death*, but I knew that was what she meant.

"Oh, don't be ridiculous, Denise. You and your family are just hysterics. You don't know the first thing about Elke. He's my friend, he would never hurt *me*. In fact, Elke is more concerned about Marguerite than most of our relatives are." I paused, conspicuously not saying *most of you*.

"For God's sake, the police should be informed! The Aurora police, and the county police, and the state police. You are not being hysterical *enough*. The detectives who interviewed Andrew and me told us to report anyone suspicious who turns up. 'Elke' is definitely suspicious."

"Don't you dare snitch to the police, Denise! I will have to strangle you again."

Laughing to show that this was just teasing.

"That isn't funny, Georgene. It wasn't funny then and it isn't funny now. Your sister has been missing for months—who knows if she's even alive. You don't seem to care. You are behaving very inappropriately."

Now, Denise was venturing too far. Now, red flames flickered over my brain.

"Don't you dare tell me if I 'care' about Marguerite! She disappeared of her own volition. No one wants to acknowledge that. She left *us*. She scorned *us*. She'd won a prize, a fancy art prize, sending her to Rome. In Italy. She was boasting at the college. Don't you dare try to tell *me*."

Laughing angrily at Denise's response, stammered fake apology, excuses, the usual ploy of seeming to agree with me then reiterating her own position, exactly the way she'd always treated me, when she took time to notice me. In a prim voice telling me she'd seen Elke's "dirty" paintings in the library. According to the local

214

paper there were complaints to the library board, the paintings were removed.

Scornfully I said: "*You* complained, probably. Admit it!"

"I—I did not. There were many complaints. Naked people, up on the walls, right there in public where children could see . . ."

"The exhibit wasn't in the children's wing. A nude portrait isn't 'dirty.'"

"Georgene, this is not like you. You are sounding like—another person . . ."

"Denise, goodnight. Thank you *so much* for your concern."

Spoken through clenched jaws. Determined to speak calmly, quietly.

But trembling badly, so that I nearly dropped the receiver as I hung up.

What I want is, to tear out your throat with my teeth. That is all.

Lena was standing in the doorway anxiously looking at me for (perhaps) I'd raised my voice after all. Determined not to slam down the receiver but (perhaps) I'd slammed it down anyhow.

That night at dinner Father noticed that I seemed to have little appetite. And I was unusually quiet. Tried to eat, truly I tried but I was distracted, excited. What I'd have liked to tell Father was exactly what I could not tell Father.

Suitor. Courting. Soul mate.

37

Waiting. But weeks would pass. Elke did not call, and Elke did not return.

Impress of his lips on the back of my hand, like a birthmark. Burning sensation in the skin.

38

Clues into the Disappearance of . . . Again, in early December 1991 Denise called. And again, in a voice quivering with indignation.

"Georgene! Have you *seen*?"

God*damn.* Wanting to quickly hang up before my cousin could spew more garbage over my head.

But this time was different, I seemed to sense. Denise's indignation did not sound cruel, rather sympathetic, even pitying.

By now, six weeks had passed. Elke had not called, and Elke had not returned. A dozen times a day in the post office I glanced up when a customer entered but it was never Elke.

No notes, no fanciful little cards. Dimly I recalled how once Elke had left a bouquet of fragrant white flowers on the front porch, and I'd been so blasé about it . . . Lena had saved the flowers from being tossed into the trash.

What I would have given now, for just a few straggly flowers from Elke.

Just a call from Elke. *Georgene?—may I come visit you, soon?*

Taste of black bile in my mouth as Denise chattered excitedly, thrillingly with some scandalous revelation involving—was it *Elke*?

Asking me if I'd seen—what?—an article in the *Ithaca Journal*?

"On the front page, Georgene! I have it right here: the headline is 'Aurora Artist's Newest Work *Clues into the Disappearance of . . .*'"

So rapidly Denise spoke, with such vehement disgust, I could barely understand what she was saying; but I knew, it was not good news.

"This 'Elke'—this horrible person you'd invited into your house—has an exhibit of new paintings in a gallery in Ithaca, 'nude portraits' of a woman resembling Marguerite, evidently! The *Journal* has published a review but there are no pictures of the exhibit because, I'm quoting here, 'the *Journal* is a family newspaper'—'frankly frontal, shockingly graphic nude portraits of a woman who seems to be bound, gagged, tortured and finally killed . . .' This is disgusting! This is actionable, I would think. Even the reviewer in the *Journal* remarks that 'Elke, known for his controversial paintings, may have overstepped ethical boundaries in his apparent exploitation of Aurora College colleague M. Fulmer, missing since last April . . .' You have to shield your father from this, Georgene! He will be outraged. We are all outraged. Imagine! How could anyone do such a vicious, vulgar thing, with Marguerite still missing! This 'Elke' has disclaimed all connection with her, of course. In interviews he's pretending that the 'beautiful blond woman-victim' in the paintings is purely invented, 'an exercise in form'—'pure figurative art.'"

This was stunning news. A total surprise. I felt as if someone had kicked me in the stomach, had to grope for a chair to sit down.

Elke—the man who'd claimed to be my "soul mate"— had betrayed me.

Marguerite, and me.

On the phone Denise's high-pitched accusatory voice continued but I did not listen. Terrible buzzing and static in my ears, I thought that I might faint.

As soon as I could I got hold of the *Ithaca Journal* and read the horrendous front-page review. As Denise said, there was no photograph of the exhibit, thank God, but there was a photograph of Elke taken in his studio in paint-splattered coveralls, glittery reptilian eyes half-closed, small smug smile inside bristling whiskers. His graying-silver hair fell in waves past his shoulders, glossy as a wig. Even the caption beneath the photograph seemed boastful: *Controversial Aurora Artist Denies "Exploitation" of Aurora Heiress Missing Since April.*

So agitated, I could not read the article straight through. Indeed, there were two articles on the front page, one a review of the exhibit coyly titled *Clues into the Disappearance of* . . . The reviewer was an art critic but, to his credit, he did not absolve Elke from "questionable ethical behavior." My eyes filled with tears as I read, reread, tried to concentrate despite a drumming in my head of utter mortification.

Rogue artist, cutting-edge, outrageous, rebel against taboos, indecent, challenging, "reconstruction" of a recent tragic event, local Aurora heiress Marguerite Fulmer, sculptress, Guggen-heim, Aurora College, insists his motives are not base, exploitive, or sexist, in the tradition of Andy Warhol, "exploring"— "parodying"—popular culture, female victim, white-blond-beautiful. Dead.

"Dead!"—the first time anyone had openly acknowledged that Marguerite might be no longer living.

How surprising it was, as well as shocking, that Elke seemed to be presenting Marguerite as *dead*. In all that he'd said to me, in our exchanges, it had seemed possible that Marguerite was only just *missing*. . . .

All the more reason to keep Father from seeing the exhibit. To keep Father from knowing about it.

And hadn't Elke been *in love* with M.? Hadn't he stared transfixed at her girlhood photographs, in Mother's albums, just a few weeks ago?

Just not possible. This must be a mistake.

◆

Telling no one exactly where I was going I hired a car to drive me to the Ithaca gallery where Elke's paintings were exhibited, to see for myself how bad this was; how scandalous, and shameful; in dark glasses and with a wide-brimmed rain hat pulled down over my head. I dreaded anyone identifying me as a relative of Marguerite Fulmer!—unlikely as that was, I could not risk it.

The first surprise: though it was a weekday afternoon the little gallery on a side street showing *Clues into the Disappearance of . . .—Oil Paintings by Elke* was not deserted as I'd hoped. Eight or nine people were crowded into the small space exhibiting six ghastly large oil canvases,

221

shameless curiosity-seekers, voyeurs; staring, at a distance of just a few inches, at a sequence of nudes obviously modeled after my sister Marguerite.

So, it was true: not exaggerated.

My disappointment was such, I realized that I'd been hoping, up until the moment I stepped into the gallery, that *Clues into the Disappearance of . . .* wasn't really about my sister but someone else. For surely—Elke could not have betrayed us . . .

The paintings were arranged in a sequence of escalating frankness, "nakedness." The first was the least offensive, a dreamlike representation of a very young woman, a girl, with a blurred beautiful face, long silver-blond hair undulating as if underwater; lying on a divan, amid precisely detailed sheets, arms and legs limp as if she were asleep, oblivious of the viewer, and of the (evident) danger she was in. Innocence, but also a kind of arrogance: that one might be so beautiful, and so brazenly display oneself, confident that no harm could befall her.

The next painting was also impressionistic but clearer now in ominous physical details: more of the face was revealed, still a beautiful face but not so young, not a girl's face, no innocence now, a hint of fine wrinkles at the eyes and the corners of the mouth, and creases in the body; a certain carelessness in the spread of legs, arms; like

222

calendar-art, the creamy breasts, belly, hips and thighs, though the naked feet were lost in shadow, and the eyes closed. By the third painting the artist's depiction of the figure had lost all pretensions of romance and had become stark, harsh, gloating, cruel: the viewer could see that the woman was in her thirties, at least; her wrists and ankles were bound with what appeared to be neckties, there was something stuffed into her mouth, the no-longer-beautiful face was contorted with terror and the rumpled linens were stained, filthy.

With each painting the woman's naked body was more cruelly exposed, with exaggerated creases in the face, throat, belly; the breasts became coarse, flaccid; the legs were hard-muscled, covered in hairs distinct as iron filings. The groin area was a scribble of pubic hair darker than the hair on the woman's head (as if M. had bleached her hair to that beautiful silvery-blond color!—an additional insult, which happened not to be true). The skin tone of the body became ever more pasty, waxen, with a greenish tinge. Some sort of damage was being inflicted in the groin area, which grew increasingly bloody, and by the final painting the ravaged body appeared to be dead, a corpse; its bones prominent, flaccid drooping breasts with curiously plastic-looking nipples, blemishes in the no longer smooth creamy skin. The gag had been removed from the anguished mouth, which had fallen open, with a fatuous look; the eyes had lost all luster, partially rolled back into the drooping head. Wrists and ankles were no longer bound but deep indentations were visible in the skin as if something other than mere cloth had been used to tie them. Fattish thighs lay limp, spread in lurid self-display.

Elke's revenge on my sister for resisting him. Elke's revenge on the Fulmers.

Viewers in the gallery were silent. If they'd come to the exhibit to be titillated, they were finding the actual experience not entertaining; fairly quickly, they hurried away, and left me alone to stare in mounting horror, disbelief.

Possibly, I had hated my sister. Even as I had (I suppose) loved her, certainly I had resented her, but I had not hated her this much. No.

What misery M. would feel, if she could know how her naked body, or rather a grotesque caricature of her naked body, was being displayed in public, in Ithaca, New York, where many people knew Marguerite Fulmer; hardly an hour's drive from her hometown, where virtually everyone knew her. Worse, her identity, which might not have been known otherwise, had been explicitly linked to Elke's exhibit by the front-page articles in the *Journal*.

(Typical media hypocrisy: castigating crude and unethical behavior like Elke's but not failing to identify the victim.)

A second viewing of the exhibit (for I forced myself!) revealed yet another obscenity: in each painting, in the lower left corner, too obscure for most viewers to notice, there lay on the floor what appeared to be a torn, discolored photograph of a young girl with blond hair . . . Now I was truly furious, for these were photographs of Marguerite which Elke must have stolen from the albums when I wasn't looking!

Each photograph mirrored the posture or pose of the nude adult woman in some way, so that the photograph, of an "innocent" girl, mocked the adult woman, unless it was the adult woman, clearly depraved, degenerate, who mocked the innocent girl.

Outrageous! Unknowing and ignorant, I had invited a thief into my father's house.

"Ma'am? Hello? Do you have any questions about the exhibit?"—a black-clad young person approached me, not evidently female, or male; thin as an eel, upright and seeming to undulate, with eyes enlarged by mascara, and a wide, membranous mouth.

"Yes. I do have questions. But I doubt that you have answers."

My voice did not quaver so much as I'd feared. Indeed, no one could have guessed how hurt, how wounded, how furious I was feeling.

Uneasily the black-clad person asked me what my questions were. Taking care to keep a little distance between us.

"My first question is: aren't you ashamed?"

"Ashamed—? Of . . ."

"Of this exhibit? Paintings of a nude, helpless woman, modeled on an actual woman from Aurora, who has been missing since April?"

"Ma'am, I only work here. This is not my gallery."

"Then you are ashamed?"

"I—I am not. No."

"Like hell, you *are*. And you should be. This is pornography, and it's disgraceful."

"Ma'am, there is no need to raise your voice. I can hear you perfectly well."

"You do not hear me *perfectly well*. You are failing to answer my question which I will repeat: are you not ashamed to be exhibiting paintings of an actual woman whom many people in this area know? Who has been 'missing'—probably a 'victim of foul play'—since last April?"

"I've said, I just work here. I don't choose the art. If you want to speak to the owner, I'll give you her card."

"*Her* card? A woman?"

"This is the 'Heidi Klein Gallery'—Mrs. Klein is the owner, and Mrs. Klein chooses the exhibits."

"Does this 'Heidi Klein' know the artist 'Elke'? Are they friends?"

"I don't know, ma'am. I'm sorry, but . . ."

"I am not leaving. Not yet. I want an answer to another question: are these paintings some sort of 'confession,' the artist is acknowledging that he has murdered the missing woman?"

"Why, I—I don't think . . . Certainly, no."

"But that's what this is, isn't it? A 'confession'?"

"These are paintings, ma'am. This is 'art.' The artist has explained that these are exercises in 'formal composition.'"

"'Exercises in formal composition!' That's a joke. These are nude bodies in paintings so large, the bodies are life-sized. The face—faces—are clearly meant to resemble an actual woman. Every blemish is highlighted. Clearly the artist hates the female body. He hates this body."

"Ma'am, I don't agree. The artist has insisted that he doesn't hate the female body, he is 'obsessed' with it. Not a particular female body—just *female*. There's an interview with him, I can give you to read . . ."

"Of course he's lying! There is the *particular* female body that's the issue here, in those paintings."

"But, as an artist—"

"—not an *artist*, a butcher. The woman in the paintings isn't known to be dead. In fact, her family has reason to believe that she's alive. So why does this 'Elke' depict her as dead? How does he know this?"

"Ma'am, Elke doesn't 'know' anything about any 'actual' woman. He's an artist, he invents. These are not photographs, or—journalism."

"Are you, or 'Heidi Klein,' aware that 'Elke' has been questioned by Aurora police? That he's a suspect in the case?"

"A 'suspect'—no. . . ."

The black-clad person's voice faltered. Knowing very well what I was talking about.

Hotly I said: "This 'Elke' may be arrested soon. Tell your employer, she may be aiding and abetting a criminal. Abduction, murder."

"Ma'am, please don't shout."

"I am *not shouting*. But I am disgusted, and I am demanding that this exhibit be shut down for reasons of public decency."

"Ma'am, I don't think—"

"There are obscenity laws, and there are certainly libel laws. 'Defamation of character.' A woman who can't defend herself is being publicly defamed."

"Are you related to her, ma'am? The woman in the painting?—the woman you think is in the painting? Is that who you are?"

"No. I am not related to Marguerite Fulmer. But I am a friend of the Fulmer family, and the family is advised to bring a suit against the 'Heidi Klein Gallery' to 'cease and desist' or suffer a lawsuit that will force it into bankruptcy."

Cease and desist. Force into bankruptcy. Such word clusters leapt from my lips! Righteous anger seized me but also a giddy elation, that left me breathless as if a great bald eagle were bearing me aloft in his talons.

Was it possible, that the exhibit could be shut down? Forced to shut down? The idea had flown into my head as I'd been envisioning how Father would react, if he knew.

If he knew, Father would certainly try to shut down the exhibit. Through threats, intimidation. In his prime, Father had never backed away from litigation.

If circumstances allowed, Father could purchase the gallery, and shut it down. Or, rather, shut down the Elke exhibit.

Failing which, what would Father do? The paintings had to be destroyed—but how?

"Ma'am, you will have to speak with Mrs. Klein. I—I can't help you any further."

"I will *strangle* Mrs. Klein! That's what I will do. Tell her."

Seeing the look in the young person's face I quickly amended, with a laugh: "I *will tangle* with Mrs. Klein. After I call my lawyer."

The black-clad young person was backing nervously away from me. As if I would care to strangle such a craven fool!

◆

Mad-glaring moon mimicking the fury of the righteous avenger. Alley at the rear of the Heidi Klein Gallery, 23 Spruce Street, Ithaca. Swirl of autumn leaves. Shadowy figure, indeterminate sex. Where a face would be, rim of a rain hat pulled low. Dark raincoat, buttoned to the neck. Dark-tinted glasses hiding hot-glaring avenger eyes.

Splashing of gasoline, gleeful-giddy against dull brick, sudden shattering of a (small, rectangular) window at a height of five feet. Entire gasoline can hurtled through the window, lighted matches following, gratifying pouf! *of flame.*

Delirium of joy, mad laughter as the obscene canvases, one by one, explode into a cataclysm of cleansing flame piercing the ceiling, the roof, streaking upward into the nighttime sky.

39

No Stone Left Unturned. No Clue Left Uninvestigated. There came then, in December 1991, the "Private Investigator" Leo Drummard into our lives.

"If my daughter is living no fee is too great to pay to find her. And if my daughter is not living, no fee is too great to find her poor remains and bring them home for a proper burial."

So Father spoke solemnly, publicly. But to no avail.

After months of frustration with the lack of progress in the police investigation(s), without my knowledge or approval in December 1991 Father hired a private investigator from Buffalo to search for her.

Poor Father! Grown desperate, making such a decision.

231

(Yes, Father had found out about "Elke," soon after the exhibit opened in Ithaca, despite my efforts to shield him. Of which more, later.)

This "PI" was a suave smooth talker (think sinister Richard Widmark in a noir film of the 1940s) whose boast was "No stone left unturned. No clue left uninvestigated." Despite his air of authority Drummard would accomplish little more than the police department(s) would accomplish with their desultory investigations, while racking up unconscionable expenses.

Whether the charlatan's name was "Leo Drummard" (as his New York State private investigator's license declared) or whether this name was a fanciful noir fabrication, I did not know; but I did not trust this person whom Father had hired as a "last resort" (Father's words) through a business associate's referral—bringing into our private life an utter stranger and allowing this stranger, one day when I was at work at the post office, to enter and search M.'s rooms, even to take photographs there!

Of course, as I had protected my sister's good name against even the possibility of scandal by hiding away, at the rear of her closet, the silky-sexy Dior slip dress that may, or may not, have been soiled with a stain of some lurid sort, so too I had busied myself, before Aurora police came to search her quarters on the morning of April 12, by

232

taking away many of the contents of M.'s drawers, leaving them neater and "better organized" than they'd been. These contents included random pieces of personal correspondence as well as M.'s 1991 desk calendar with diary-like notations on many of the days, initials, times, places; most of this, I was sure, had to be perfectly innocuous, and innocent; but buried within the commonplace, who knew what clues to secrets in M.'s life, which M. would not have wished known?

For instance, the medical appointments.

I'd noticed them immediately. For they were suspicious, to me.

March 29, April 8. On the first date, an appointment for "MAM" at 11 A.M.; on the second, at 9 A.M.

(Surely these indicated mammograms. Had to be at the Ithaca radiology center, the very place to which our mother had gone at the time of receiving her [lethal] diagnosis of stage three breast cancer.)

And again, on April 9, a notation in tiny script, virtually unreadable: *not* MAM but BIO. 8:30 A.M.

Biopsy? Possibly.

The most tantalizing clues come slantwise. You must decipher them slantwise. Not if they are genuine clues into the disappearance of my sister but if, to the detective-mind, *they will be so interpreted.*

233

None of this did I want Drummard to see. Vulgar speculations about my sister, inquiries at the clinic in Ithaca. I was certain that none of the (male) investigators assigned to the case ever knew about the clinic—I'd made sure, by taking the calendar. None of their business. M.'s body was no one's business, not even mine.

Inhabiting a female body is such a feat for me, like squeezing into a costume that includes a perfectly fitted face mask through which it is quite a feat to breathe, I try not to think of it; try not to think of how Mother in her female body confronted her diagnosis, the (futile) treatments that followed, and finally her death.

None of my business. I. Do. Not. Wish. To. Know.

So, the calendar is gone. Letters, cards, personal items, tossed into the dumpster behind the post office and long ago hauled away to a landfill.

(No, I did not dispose of M.'s sketchbook with these but hid it away in a safe space where the likes of Drummard would never find it. My calculations were, I might one day be named the executrix of M. Fulmer's estate and would be approached as an "expert" in M. Fulmer's art; I would then reveal to an astonished world that M. Fulmer had sketched a number of fine pencil and charcoal drawings, attesting to a talent that went beyond the "classicism" of her sculpture.)

So, by the time busybody "Leo Drummard" appeared on the scene not a thing remained in M.'s part of the house that might have been interpreted, or misinterpreted, as a "clue" to her disappearance.

◆

"Well, Mr. Drummard," I said, my voice as heavy with sarcasm as my eyebrows were thick, dark, and heavy, meeting like furry caterpillars at the bridge of my nose, "—did you find anything 'of interest' in my sister's rooms?" and Mr. Drummard glared at me and said, "Miss Fulmer, I think you know the answer to that question, don't you," and I said, demurely, resisting the impulse to laugh in the fool's face, "Why yes, Mr. Drummard, I believe that I do."

Sensing discord between us, though perplexed at its source, Father glanced from Drummard to me, and back again, but could not guess what the issue was, any more than Drummard could have claimed *without a shadow of a doubt* that, indeed, I had cleared away from my sister's rooms any "clues" that might have interested him, or the police.

However, when Drummard requested permission to search our entire house, attic to cellar, I overruled Father by saying vehemently: "No, sir. You will not."

235

Drummard protested: "But, Miss Fulmer, how am I to investigate your sister's disappearance if . . ."

"You can be sure, Mr. Drummard, that my sister is *not in this house*. If you'd done your homework you would know that my sister's wallet was discovered on a country road months ago and the consensus among professionals is that she was *abducted by force*. Therefore, she is likely to be somewhere far away from here. Hardly in this house."

"But, Miss Fulmer—"

"Not in this house! And this house is precious to us, we can't allow it to be violated by strangers."

Seeing that I was unusually agitated, Father supported my position. Like Marguerite, though not like Mother, he'd learned to placate and humor me if my voice rose an octave, and if the issue was not one he felt strongly about. Telling Drummard, in a reasonable voice, that if we'd discovered anything in the house that would have been helpful to the police investigations, we'd certainly have told the detectives; but there hadn't been.

"I see. Hmm."

Drumming his fingers on the armrest of his chair, poor dummy-Drummard. His face was that of a man of youthful but rapidly aging middle-age, an ex-athlete, perhaps, no longer muscular but fleshy, fibrous; once handsome, accustomed to silly women casting him wistful glances, retaining still a ridiculous little mustache on his upper lip, too dark to be natural; while the hair on his head, unconvincingly wavy, and thick, smelling of a particularly repellent hair oil, had grayed like something left in the rain.

Burst capillaries in his nose, a secret drinker. Faint odor wafting from his "dapper" clothing, stale cigar smoke.

Well: not so secret a drinker, for Drummard raised his glass to sip Father's whisky with a look of barely restrained thirst.

We were in the drawing room where for the past hour he and Father had been talking earnestly. Drummard had plied Father with routine questions about M. while I observed, mostly silent, staring at the man in a way to unnerve him, for I knew that the "private investigator" was not my friend.

Already the charlatan is suspicious of YOU.

Never will he dare acknowledge this suspicion to Father.

And never will it come to anything. YOU *need not worry.*

It made me smile that Drummard had been flummoxed by M.'s rooms: absolutely nothing out of place, everything neat and clean and organized, closets and drawers conspicuously orderly, and nothing *of interest*.

In this, Lena was my co-conspirator. Encouraged by me to clean M.'s rooms regularly even though M. was no longer inhabiting them. No cobwebs would accumulate, no thin layer of dust. Sink, mirror above sink, bathroom tile floor sparkling-clean, as M. would wish.

Opened windows, fresh air. No stale air to remind us of her absence.

Time to leave, was it? I'd been willing Drummard out of his chair and on his way so that Father and I could have our usual pleasant dinner together at the dining room table, served by Lena.

Tonight, Thursday: brisket of beef slow-cooked with parsnips, baby onions. Father's (favorite) lime Jell-O molded dessert with oatmeal biscuits.

(Did Drummard smell the delicious aromas wafting from Lena's kitchen? Did his mouth water, did his steely eyes soften, did his brittle-bachelor soul begin to melt just a little anticipating an invitation from Father, to *stay, and have dinner with us* and, less likely, yet still not totally impossibly, an impulsive invitation from Miss Fulmer—*Oh yes, please stay, we would love you to join us*? I hope so: for so the man's hopes would be dashed.)

"If you change your mind, Mr. Fulmer, about allowing me to search the entire house, let me know"—these words of Drummard were directed exclusively toward Father, bypassing me entirely; a gesture of such rudeness, I

238

wonder that Father didn't react; but of course Father is too gentlemanly to react in such circumstances.

Coldly I replied: "We are not going to change our mind, Mr. Drummard. What we expect from you, at the prices you dare to charge, is to investigate Marguerite's disappearance in a professional manner, without bothering us. We are hoping that you can complete the *woefully incomplete police investigation* and find her."

These clipped words of mine provoked Drummard to glare at me in fury: male indignation, impotence, fury.

But he dared not utter an impudent syllable since Father was present, and Father was his employer.

"Miss Fulmer, that is exactly what I intend to do."

Pushing a fedora onto his blunt bullet-head, like a "PI" in a noir film. Taking his leave of us by shaking Father's hand gravely but only just nodding brusquely to me, steely eyes averted.

Puckishly, I saw Drummard to the front door. Bade him farewell, good luck, and goodbye.

Observing from a leaded-glass window in the foyer the private investigator stiff-striding out the front walk to his car (showy Buick, of a bygone year) parked at the curb.

Silly man!—as if he could threaten *me*.

40

Highway of Tears. Nonetheless, Drummard brought surprises into my life!—for all my opposition to the man, and my contempt for him.

Let me state plainly: I saw Leo Drummard *just that single time* in December 1991. With Father in our drawing room at the outset of the PI's (futile) investigation sprawling over seven billable months and how many thousands of dollars, I cannot imagine.

(The cagey PI communicated exclusively with Father, calling him at his office in town, or at times of the day when I was not home and could not listen on the phone extension even if I'd overcome my scruples against eavesdropping. Despite the generous retainer Father had given him there were myriad expenses which Drummard asked

Father to wire to him, as he traveled about New York State staying in first-class hotels; always "additional" or "unanticipated" expenses.)

(Yes, I did plead with Father not to pay the last of Drummard's submitted bills; but, Father being a gentleman, he would hear nothing of the sort.)

Yet, from this questionable personality we would be informed of astonishing information that police detectives never troubled to report to us: that there had been, at the time of M.'s disappearance, numerous women and girls who'd (also) disappeared but had been found subsequently and identified, many of them suffering from amnesia; women who'd turned up in places unfamiliar to them, as victims of (evident) assault; unable to remember their assailants, or even what had happened to them.

In some cases unable to remember their own names.

These were women and girls diagnosed as amnesia victims; it was speculated that they'd been (originally) victims of abductions whose abductors had decided, for whatever reason, not to murder but to free them.

So many!—amnesiac victims, female, who might have been M., but were not; whose pictures, faxed to us by the intrepid Drummard, bore some resemblance to M.

In fact, in all fairness to Drummard, some of these women *closely resembled* M. Only a close relative might perceive that the features in the faxed picture were not identical to those of our missing Marguerite; not quite so silvery-blond as M., not so beautiful nor so "patrician" as M.

Indeed, the Pfeiffer woman, the absurd *psychic voyager,* had told us of "missing persons" but without such descriptions; in the astrologist's cosmology, there were no broken minds or bodies. Drummard, the *private investigator,* took us to a very different place.

It was his practice, Drummard boasted, to travel about from place to place with a folder of photographs of the missing person he sought, to show to local police and to compare with photographs on file with the police. He did not trust, he said, "new-fangled" devices like fax machines and computers though, in certain circumstances, he had no choice but to use them.

An exacting, old-fashioned sort of methodology, costing Father a good deal.

*No stone left unturned! No clue left uninvestigated!—*Drummard had a most maddening way of boasting with a downward cast of his features, like a Christian martyr at the stake.

More upsetting than the amnesiac victims were the plenitude of (unidentified) female corpses Drummard unearthed, in a manner of speaking: discovered in remote rural areas of New York State; in vacant lots and alleys in cities and towns; in parks, in forests, by roadsides; in shallow graves, and in landfills; in the trunks of abandoned vehicles and in boarded-up buildings; washed ashore, bobbing beneath rotted docks on rivers and lakes; occasionally in plain, shocking view in public places: park, square, highway, cemetery, the steps of churches and of City Halls. Invariably, if ungallantly, these luckless women were described as "poor"—"mentally ill"—"suspected prostitute."

All too often, Drummard made a discovery that made our blood run cold. For instance, a few weeks after M.'s disappearance the naked body of a woman of M.'s approximate age and physical type was discovered in Alcott, New York, on a littered beach of Lake Ontario; so badly decomposed that identification could be made only through an examination of dental work, which required a week's time before Father and I were notified that the remains were not M.'s . . .

Grisly relief! To be grateful that someone else's daughter and sister has died, not your own.

All this, the (transparent, to me) effort of Drummard to assure us that he was working very hard, dredging up such horrors, as if such horrors might cast light upon M.'s disappearance, in turn justifying Drummard for charging

Father an extravagant fee. Each day, faxed material came to us, dreaded, unwanted, an inexhaustible nightmare of female victims: bludgeoned to death in bathtubs, and in basements; shot at point-blank range in the face; stabbed "multiple times" and left to bleed to death at campsites, or in parking lots at the rear of taverns or fast-food restaurants; bodies doused with gasoline, so burnt that nothing remained but a few charred bones, teeth; floating in the Mohawk River at Troy, in a campsite in the Adirondacks, at the outskirts of the village of Lake Skaneateles, the most "scenic" of the Finger Lakes (less than an hour's drive from Cayuga Lake). There was the figure of pathos "Jane Doe"—a disarticulated skeleton discovered buried in the earthen floor of a dairy barn near Middleport, believed to have belonged to a girl of about fifteen, who might have died a decade before; another "Jane Doe," a woman of about forty, garroted, bizarrely preserved in a storage locker, wrapped in airtight plastic, in Syracuse.

And these were just *unidentified female bodies* found in upstate New York within a narrow span of time.

In this way I learned of the notorious "Highway of Tears"—a 450-mile rural stretch of Highway 16 between Prince George and Prince Rupert, British Columbia, Canada—where the bodies of dozens of women, most of them aboriginal, have been found between 1970 and the present; and of equally notorious I-35 running north-south through Oklahoma and Texas where for decades the bodies of numerous women and girls, many of them never identified, have been dumped by the wayside. *The earth is bloody with the bodies of raped, murdered, cast-aside women and girls.*

Zealous Drummard looked into criminal cases in New York State that had been adjudicated, forcing Father and me into an unwanted familiarity with "sexual predators"—"sexual sadists"—"serial sexual killers"—that could have no bearing upon M.'s case, or so it seemed to me; an excess of information, to smother objections to Drummard's expense account.

One of these "suspects" was a forty-three-year-old drifter known as the "Wolf's Head Lake Killer," convicted in November 1991 of abducting, raping, torturing, and murdering two young women at Wolf's Head Lake (in the Adirondacks), in the late 1980s, serving two consecutive life sentences at the Clinton Maximum Security Facility in Dannemora, New York, whom Drummard made an effort to link to M.'s disappearance on the basis of very slim evidence, that did not convince state police to reopen their investigation; another, a similar felon already found guilty of abduction and murder, serving a life sentence at Attica. Both these persons might have been in the vicinity of Aurora on April 11, 1991, Drummard argued. Either *might* have encountered Marguerite Fulmer hiking along Drumlin Road that morning . . .

These felons, and others, Drummard unearthed in his campaign to leave *no stone unturned*. Initially, Father may have been drawn into Drummard's enthusiasm for rummaging through the stinking dumpster of convicted sexual sadists in New York state prisons; but soon then, Father grew suspicious of the effort, though (to my disappointment) he continued to support Drummard, being reluctant to *give up the search for Marguerite*.

But I knew better: I was the voice of reason, caution. Explaining to Father that when a serial killer is apprehended, law enforcement officers try to blame him for numerous murders so that they can close their cases; in certain egregious situations, a cunning killer can "confess" to murders he hasn't committed in order to make a deal with authorities for a lighter sentence, or a sentence in a less notorious prison. Drummard was hoping to tie one of the convicted killers to my sister's disappearance—very conveniently! Though no body would ever be found, yet the culprit could be named, and the case "closed"—at least, to a degree.

Did private investigators and local police sometimes strike deals together?—were local prosecutors susceptible to deals, as well? Did money change hands? *I would not trust any of these people, whose livelihoods depend upon crime and criminals and making deals with them.*

How cruel they are, who trade upon the hope of parents, that their lost children will be restored to them! That some "closure" might be found. Cynical, and monstrous—I seethed with resentment of Leo Drummard who continued to hint to Father that he wanted to search our house "attic to cellar."

Over my dead body.

◆

All that Drummard stirred into consciousness has not settled, more than twenty years later.

For it was during the months of Drummard that I'd begun lying awake in my bed at night thinking of the female victims whose photographs he faxed to us with numbing frequency: strangers who (often, uncannily) resembled M., sisters (of a kind). Never before had I seriously thought of other girls and women as *sisters* for it was enough (it was more than enough!) to have my own older *sister.*

Thinking *So many! How has God allowed so many?*

Thinking how, if things had been just slightly otherwise, M.'s corpse could be among them. *Or my own.*

More to placate my own unease, than to prepare myself for any plausible assault in Father's fortified house, I'd begun keeping a very sharp, serrated butcher knife in a bedside drawer.

Reasoning: if I never needed this knife, good. And if I ever needed it: thank God!

41

Drummard vs. Elke. Unavoidably, this would come to pass.

All that shame, humiliation, and mortification which I'd hoped to keep from Father was summarily presented to him in one of Drummard's reports: that the *artist-in-residence* at Aurora College, M.'s own colleague, who'd claimed to be a close friend of hers, had had an exhibit in December in an Ithaca gallery of "shockingly graphic" nude paintings of a woman who closely resembled her, suggesting that M. had been murdered by strangulation; that the paintings had been priced between $13,600 and $16,500, and *had all sold.*

Outrageous, disgusting! That such obscene art had been *sold.*

For of course, I hadn't had the courage to throw a container of gasoline into the Heidi Klein Gallery and set it aflame. I hadn't the courage to file a complaint with Ithaca authorities, that the exhibit should be shut down: I knew that it would not be, and I'd only make a fool of myself and call yet more attention to the obscenity.

A vague notion had come to me, that I might purchase the paintings myself that hadn't yet been sold, and destroy them, using my trust fund allowance; but the idea was loathsome to me. For Elke would be absurdly proud, to have sold out the entire exhibit within a few days; and I would not want the information to get back to him, that the Fulmers had bought out the exhibit, for he would simply paint more, with a motive of blackmail.

Hadn't Elke boasted that he could "easily" forge a copy of the Ryder painting? So, too, Elke could "easily" replicate the nude portraits of *Clues into the Disappearance of . . .* since the artwork was so crude, sensational.

Still, it was hard to believe that Elke had betrayed *me*, even if he'd betrayed *her*.

Following the largely negative publicity in the wake of the exhibit, Elke had been once again questioned by detectives but again, lacking evidence that might justify an arrest, detectives had had to let Elke go; he'd vehemently denied any involvement in M.'s disappearance, insisting that his art was "purely formal, experimental" and that the depiction of a strangled blond woman, a corpse, in the last painting in the exhibit had no relationship to anything in the actual world: "Figures in paintings are not 'bodies' but representations of bodies. An artist paints what is in *him*, not in the world."

Still, Aurora residents had come to believe that Elke *was* involved in M.'s disappearance, including even Elke's (estranged) wife and two adolescent children, living now in Syracuse, and refusing all requests for interviews.

(Yes: most embarrassingly, Elke turned out to be *married*.)

(I have to confess, I was stunned by this revelation. Married! Father of two children! Nothing had seemed less likely than that Elke, of all people, would have succumbed to a *domestic arrangement*.)

Drummard reported that, under pressure from the Aurora College board of trustees, on which Father had served generously for more than thirty years, Elke had resigned his position at Aurora College for a "controversial" settlement. He'd moved away from Aurora to live in a studio apartment on West 24th Street, New York City, close by the "chic" Chelsea Gallery that had offered him a contract for new work.

(Moved away! So, I would never see him again, probably. No chance for Elke to apologize to *me*.)

251

As it happened, Elke's disgusting exhibit in Ithaca, initially denounced as "misogynist pornography," had been brought to the gallery in Chelsea to be re-examined by art critics for the *New York Times* and *Art News*, recognized now as a "bold revisiting" of the cartoon art of Philip Guston and a "hard-edged realism" exploring the "sexual politics of body horror"; like Cindy Sherman and Andy Warhol, Elke was said to be "parodying the fetishism" of the female body. Where mainstream feminist reviewers had reviled the artist for his "exploitation" of a female artist, radical feminist reviewers were applauding him for his "unflinching examination" of the "broken, mutilated female body" that was a familiar "trope" in American popular culture.

It was even rumored that collectors were commissioning Elke for new work that continued the obsessions of *Clues into the Disappearance of.* . . . Drummard had heard that prices were in the range of $200,000–$500,000.

"The cad! I could murder him with my bare hands!"—Father said bitterly; but with such an air of resignation, I understood that nothing would come of it.

42

The Premonition. On a weekday afternoon in February 1992 returning early from the Mill Street post office with a complaint of "flu symptoms"—(which complaint rarely invites distrust or disbelief, rather more an eagerness to be rid of the stricken one)—I discovered, in the house, a disturbed air; an odor, unmistakable, of stale cigar smoke, and hair oil; in Lena's expression, alarm, and guilt.

"Is someone in the house, Lena? Is it—'Drummard'?"

Now frightened, Lena told me *yes.* My father had given Drummard permission to search the house, at such a time when I wasn't on the premises.

This was a shock. This was a revelation. That Father conspired behind my back not only with Drummard, but with Lena.

No one to trust! Not even Father, from now on.

But calmly I said: "I see. Well—perhaps it's for the best. Father does *know best*."

In this way totally deceiving Lena, for the woman could have no idea of the rage that burned in my heart; rather, Lena felt sympathy for me, that Father had gone behind my back to allow the interloper into the house, in defiance of my advice.

"And where is he now? I hope—not in my room!"

Hurriedly Lena assured me that Drummard had promised not to search my room but "only to peep" into it; so far as she was aware he'd finished with most of the rooms and might be in the basement now.

"Well. I will be sure to avoid the basement."

Taking my leave of Lena who was looking, at this point, vastly relieved.

An uneasy premonition had brought me home in midafternoon. A sense of foreboding, unease. A bad night the previous night, imagining I heard footsteps in the house, in the vicinity of M.'s room.

But never do I investigate these "footsteps." *I do not give in.*

In a way, it was not so surprising that the manipulative "PI" had convinced Father to allow him his search. It was not surprising but it was a profound shock, as if the

charlatan had dared to smirk in my face, in acknowledg-
ment that we were mortal enemies.

No stone unturned. No clue uninvestigated.

Evidently Father himself was not home. This seemed,
to me, a very significant sign.

(Yes, since M.'s disappearance, I have come to believe
in "signs"—specifically, signs sent to *me*, indecipherable
to anyone else.)

After an innocuously pleasant exchange with Lena
during which it was revealed that she was planning, for
our evening meal, one of Father's favorite dinners (roast
leg of lamb with rosemary-roasted baby potatoes, melted
onions, and homemade apple sauce), I departed the
kitchen with Lena smiling after me, vastly relieved that
I did not appear to be upset; took the back stairs to the
second floor, to my room, walking in my (usual) heavy-
heeled manner, that couldn't fail to impress itself upon
Lena, as nothing out of the ordinary. There, in my room,
I removed the sharp-serrated butcher knife from the
bedside drawer—(which, if Drummard had discovered,
he'd left untouched)—and hid it in my clothes; from my
room, with unusual lightness and stealth I made my way
to the front stairs, and down, and along the corridor to
the rear of the house, blithe as a shadow. No one heard:
no one saw.

There, the door to the basement was open and the light was on. A faint odor of cigar and hair oil wafted to my sensitive nostrils.

"The cad! I could murder him with my bare hands."

(Who uttered these words? I am not sure. Yet, I heard them clearly.)

Laughing, heart beating hard with the exhilaration of purpose, I very quietly descended the stairs into the nether region below, unvisited, by me, since July of the previous year.

PART III

43

Anniversary. Each year on April 11 there continue to appear, in those small-town newspapers still published in the Finger Lakes region of New York State, brief acknowledgments of the anniversary of my sister's disappearance. Initially, these pieces appeared on the front page of the papers; by degrees, over the years, they have gravitated toward the inner pages.

> *Investigation into Missing Aurora Heiress Stalled*
> *Police Concede "No Leads"*

And—

> *Family of Aurora Heiress Missing Since April 1991*
> *"Still Hopeful"*

(For indeed, Father remains stubbornly "still hopeful.")

Often, there is an accompanying "human interest" interview for in Aurora there remain many persons who'd known Marguerite: former teachers and classmates, old friends and friend-claimants, neighbors and college colleagues, virtually everyone and anyone with a random memory and a few maudlin remarks to usher into print. Even M.'s former piano teacher Mrs. Lomax, fondly recalling the seventeen-year-old's "talent for the piano" and "sweet personality"; even one of the (now-retired) Cayuga County detectives, recalling the "most challenging" case of his career, that "haunts me to this day."

Sentimental, trite musings: "That beautiful talented young woman artist, all of her life before her, and whoever did it—never found. So much evil in the world."

"We pray for Marguerite. We have not forgotten!"

Same old photo of Marguerite taken in her early twenties. Unlike the rest of us, M. never ages.

Missing since April 11, 1991. Voluminous police files. Investigation never closed.

44

Clue No Clue.

Not sure why but: the other day, I decided to look up Walter Lang.

Years after the fact. But what *was* the fact?

◆

Surprising that Walter Lang, once so promising a young research scientist at Cornell, is on the faculty at Rensselaer Polytechnic in nearby Troy, New York.

"All these years. So close! We might have commiserated."

(Often, I speak aloud. Not to myself so much as to the air. If anyone is listening? Recording? For now, in the 21st century, there are said to be surveillance video cameras everywhere.)

Impulsively, I hired a young nephew to drive me, two hundred miles to the city of Troy. On the condition that the transaction is kept confidential: no gossiping about (eccentric) Aunt Georgene to the relatives.

At the age of forty-five often I regret that I'd never learned to drive. I have no driver's license, and no vehicle of my own. (M.'s Volvo is still in the garage and might be resuscitated after twenty-two years if anyone cared to make the effort.) Yes: I regret not having tried harder to learn to drive; not giving up so soon, when driving instructors expressed impatience with me, or outright fear of me behind the wheel. When you are young, your every vexation seems significant, to be indulged by others as well as yourself. When you are not so young, these youthful vexations begin to seem but stupid mistakes.

For a brief while when I was in high school M. tried to teach me but soon became exasperated like my other instructors.

"Oh, Gigi! You seem to *want* to scrape Father's car."

That was not true. I insist, it *was not*.

Of course, there is a car service in Aurora which I can use if I wish, as well as my young nephew. Father still drives, though not after dusk; his eyesight has dimmed, even as his mind remains as sharp, or nearly as sharp, as ever.

After the hilly gothic beauty of the fabled Cornell campus, the brusque urban setting of Rensselaer Poly-technic was something of a shock to me. For, all these years, I'd been imagining Walter Lang still at Cornell.

And such a swarm of students! I felt a certain loss: a sinking of the heart.

From a little distance I observed Professor Lang emerging from a lecture hall: grown heavyset, shorter than I recalled, bifocal glasses blinking in dull winter sunshine.

Had I not ascertained beforehand when, and where, Professor Lang would be lecturing that morning, I might not have recognized the man. For he'd lost his wiry dark hair. He'd lost the affably awkward manner of Fred MacMurray. Descending steps with the caution of a man no longer young who must be careful of his knees, his back.

But then, I was no longer an audacious young Katharine Hepburn. Indeed, not even an audacious middle-aged Katharine Hepburn.

The romantic comedy had not caught fire, who knows why? Our fates are decided, cruelly, irrevocably, by the screenplays that narrate them, of which we have no aware-ness, still less control.

263

Carrying a battered leather briefcase that looked impracticably heavy. Kindly-faced, fretful-eyed. No doubt, once-youthful Walter Lang had dwindled into a dutiful husband, father. In his early fifties by now (I calculated) and so his children are (probably) grown. (And whom did Walter marry, having lost the love of his life?)

Or has his life rushed by him, like a spring torrent? Or crept by him, like a broken-backed snake? Like mine?

You never gave me a chance, Walter. No one has given me a chance.

She was in the way.

She was (always) in the way.

My foolish heart was beating hard, quickly.

"Excuse me? Professor Lang? Walter? I wonder if you remember me"—with a giddy rush of enthusiasm I addressed the man, stunned by my own courage.

Professor Lang was startled, for a moment blinking and staring; then, smiling at me, uncertainly.

"I—I'm not sure . . . Were you a student of mine, at Cornell?"

I was tempted to say *yes*. Blushing, flattered.

"I'm afraid not, no. I didn't attend Cornell. I was—I am—the sister of a woman you once knew. A younger sister . . ."

Walter Lang stared at me baffled. For I was clearly not a *younger sister* now but a woman of sturdy middle age, in dull-winter browns, booted feet, with nostrils visibly reddened from a cold, and swollen ankles.

". . . Marguerite Fulmer? You might remember her . . ."

Now Walter Lang's expression altered. Tightened. A wary look in the eyes, a shrinkage of the mouth.

"Oh. I see. 'Marguerite Fulmer.'"

Flat voice, flat affect. If a mannequin could speak, it would speak like this.

Hurriedly I said: "When I'd met you, when you knew Marguerite, you'd come to visit my father in Aurora. When Marguerite was in New York City. You—you were wondering what had happened to Marguerite, she'd left 'without saying goodbye' to you." Short of breath I paused, faint-headed as my heart raced. If only Walter Lang didn't stare so *sternly* at me. "At the time you were at Cornell. I'd always thought of you at Cornell. It was surprising to me, to discover that you're here at Rensselaer Polytechnic . . ."

Tactless of me, I suppose. How I was chattering, nervously!

A look of irony came over Walter's face, like a cobwebbed mask. His lips twitched into a sneer.

265

"Well. For years I was a 'suspect' in Marguerite Fulmer's disappearance. As you might know, if you are Marguerite's sister."

"A 'suspect' . . . ? I don't think so."

"Not an *official* suspect. But *de facto*. I was never arrested, there were never charges brought against me, so I couldn't clear my name. As far as I know no one was ever arrested. And Marguerite was never found—is that correct?"

He doesn't say "Marguerite's body." He thinks of her as living too.

"That's right. Marguerite was never 'found.'"

"The case is still open?"

"The case is still 'open.'"

There'd sprung between us an immediate intimacy, painful to each of us. I was sure that Walter Lang must feel it, as keenly as I did.

"So, who did you say you are? The 'younger sister'?"

"Georgene. We've met. . . ."

When you came to our house searching for Marguerite but found me instead.

Stiff-faced, unsmiling, Walter Lang considered me, with no (evident) sign of recognition. Yet, I was sure that he knew exactly who I was.

"And you've come to see me—why, exactly?"

"I—I just wanted—to see how you are . . ."

"To see how I *am*?" Walter Lang laughed, bitterly. "As you can see, I'm alive. In a manner of speaking. 'This is Hell, nor am I out of it.' Is that what you'd wanted to know?"

"No! Not at all. I—I've felt sorry for . . . I've wondered . . ."

My voice trailed off, I had no idea what I was saying. It was not true that I'd been thinking of Walter, not for years. In a way, I'd imagined him still as a young man in his thirties, at Cornell; in another way, I'd imagined him no longer living.

As my sister is both alive, and no longer living. Not for years.

"No one ever apologized to me, for destroying my life," Walter said. "And all because I'd fallen in love with Marguerite Fulmer, and wanted to marry her. What a joke!"

But why was it a *joke*? I didn't want to hear this.

Bitterly Walter continued: "There was no evidence at all to suggest that I'd 'abducted' Marguerite. Nothing. I spent most of my waking hours in the lab, as others could attest. But I was questioned by Cayuga County police, and by New York State police, repeatedly. I was brought to police headquarters for questioning, and kept overnight in 'detention,' with petty criminals and mentally ill persons, and then I was released; brought again and

267

questioned, and again kept overnight, and released. The strategy was to wear me down, so that I would 'confess.' Though I had nothing to 'confess.' People who knew me were questioned. My professors, at Cornell. My colleagues. Even my lab students. My own parents, my neighbors! I had to hire a lawyer—eventually, lawyers. I went into debt—thousands of dollars. I became a nervous wreck. I couldn't concentrate on my work. I couldn't sleep. When my three-year contract ran out at Cornell it wasn't renewed. There'd come a shadow over my life like a shadow in an X-ray, metastasizing cancer."

Walter paused, wiping roughly at his eyes.

"And all because I'd fallen in love with your sister, who hadn't given a damn about me."

"But—that's not true. Marguerite had feelings for you . . ."

" 'Feelings!' Did she!"

On all sides young people were streaming past us without so much as glancing at us, as if we were invisible. Virtually all were young men, husky, hurried, wearing backpacks, a mixture of skin tones, not predominantly "white."

Amid them, middle-aged Walter Lang and I were likely to appear pasty-skinned, as of another era, another century.

It had never occurred to me: that anyone undeserving, apart from me, might have suffered because of M. For love of M.

I wanted to say something to lift Walter's spirits but could not think what this might be.

". . . I was engaged to another young woman, a few years later. But when she learned that I was still a 'person of interest' in the Fulmer case, she broke off the engagement. My entire life has been ruined by . . ."

"Walter, I am sorry!"

Walter. This intimacy between us, a vise tightening around my chest. In a certain sort of scene, we might stumble together at this moment, to embrace; I might close my arms around the unhappy man, to console him. But Walter remained stiff and unyielding on the step above me, with no inclination to step down.

"For a long time I thought about her constantly. I was mourning her—I did love her. That I was terrorized for having known her never turned me against *her*. By now she's been declared dead, yes? After seven years?"

"Yes. Seven years."

"But there is no proof that she is actually—*dead* . . ."

"No. No proof."

There was a pause. Walter Lang was looking haggard, exhausted. As if he'd had enough of this and wanted now desperately to escape.

Quickly I asked: "Did you ever give Marguerite gifts? There were things in her possession we couldn't identify."

269

"Gifts? I don't think so."

"Jewelry? Clothes?"

"A book, maybe. A book or two. I seem to recall—Lewis Carroll, *The Hunting of the Snark*. Was that it?"

Was that it! Here was an entirely new and unexpected bit of information, not a clue, something less than a clue, perhaps an anti-clue. For a moment I was stymied, how to reply.

"I—I don't know. I don't remember *The Hunting of the Snark*."

"I might have given a copy to Marguerite but—I think, yes—she left it behind in my car . . . I didn't have money to give her anything substantial. I was just a post-doc living on a stipend. It became obvious quickly that Marguerite had much more money than I did, and that made things awkward between us. She insisted upon paying for her own meals when we went out. 'I can afford to pay my own way,' she said. I'd felt hurt, actually. But I was grateful for her thoughtfulness. I saw later, in retrospect, that 'M. Fulmer' was just too special, for me. Beyond my reach. Her sculptures, her life. I was reaching too high, like Icarus. And I was swatted down like a fly."

"Oh! Don't say that."

Pressing my hand against my breast. My heart hurt.

Walter Lang, a casualty of my sister. Collateral damage, in the drama of her life. The poor man had invented a narrative to explain his life: the lost possibilities of his life.

It was not an accurate narrative. Yet, I could not have explained to him why it was not.

"You were the victim of chance, Walter. You weren't reaching 'too high.' My father liked you . . ."

"He did? He *did*?"

"Don't you remember, he called you 'son'?"

"No . . ."

How strange, that I would remember, and Walter Lang would not. Unless I was misremembering out of sentiment.

And now he will ask: how is your father? May I visit him again?

But Walter seemed confused, at a loss for words. For the first time he seemed actually to be looking directly at me. Seeing *me*.

Now I dared to ask him the question I had prepared: "Did you ever give Marguerite a Dior dress?"

"'Dior dress'? What's that?"

"Dior—a famous designer. I think French."

Walter shook his head *no*. Now he was smiling, wryly.

"I doubt that Marguerite would have allowed a gift like that. Not that it was too expensive but that it was too intimate. Marguerite had a problem with intimacy . . . I

271

suppose I did too. Though now that I think of it, she liked to shop in thrift shops in Ithaca. Secondhand stores, antique shops. She liked to look for cast-off things. She'd laugh saying that people thought she spent money on luxury clothing when in fact she paid very little for her clothes, in high-end 'consignment' shops."

"Really! I didn't know that."

(But had I known it? Possibly.)

Not a part of M.'s personality I cared to dwell upon: her frugal nature. Far easier to dislike my sister, thinking of her spending money on luxury items.

"I remember now, we were walking along the street. She took me into one of these thrift shops. She could be lighthearted, fun. Like a girl. She looked through 'designer clothes'—expensive things marked down to a fraction of what they'd cost originally. Maybe what she bought that day was a 'Dior' . . ."

"What did it look like? Was it white?"

"I think it might have been—but very silky-white, a kind of shiny white. Yes."

"A 'slip dress'—very short, with spaghetti straps?"

Slip dress. Spaghetti straps.

How bizarre, to be recalling something so trivial, at such a time in our lives.

"You're looking surprised," Walter said hesitantly.

To which I replied, with a forced laugh, "Not *me.*"

Disappointed, yes. Clue no clue after all these years.

Grim snow-swept pavement, urban campus of a tech college. Walter Lang grown heavyset and middle-aged who had long lingered in my imagination as boyish, tender-wounded, staring at me with anguished eyes on the walkway in front of our house. And Father calling him *son.*

Now, a look of defeat about Walter's shoulders, body heavy with gravity.

"Yes, Marguerite liked 'bargains.' She could be playful. She didn't like to discuss her sculptures but she did tell me once that they, too, were 'playful'—'games.' One day, I remember, she bought me a necktie in a store on State Street—something silky too, a designer tie. Marked down from one hundred dollars to twenty dollars." Walter smiled sadly, recalling. "But I rarely wore it. Too fancy for me."

Such intimacy between us! A tremor coursed through me, I was gathering courage just to touch Walter's arm, his wrist.

So much to say to each other!—having just discovered each other, after so many years.

We would walk together in a park, talking earnestly. The Mohawk River was nearby, I'd noticed an esplanade beside it. We would have a meal together that evening. We would speak of the past frankly and unflinchingly. For it seemed that Walter Lang wasn't married after all. He had no wife awaiting him, he had no children. We would weep together for the beautiful young woman we'd both lost. We would console each other.

I would send my nephew back home for the night, I would spend the night in a hotel in Ithaca.

Tenderly Walter would say: "Thank you, Georgene. For coming into my life after so many years of loneliness."

And I would say: "I hope it isn't too late, Walter."

"It is never too late to discover a soul-mate. Marguerite would be happy for us."

But when I suggested a walk, away from the busy campus so that we could talk more privately, Walter declined with a vehement jerk of his head. He had two dozen lab notebooks to correct, he said.

Now he was speaking more brusquely. As if waking, rousing himself from a trance. No longer looking at me but beyond me. With an air of impatience.

I suggested "drinks"—"coffee"—in a place nearby? But no, Walter had no more time right now, he had the lab books to correct, also a lecture to prepare for the next day: three courses each term, his teaching load, no longer a research scientist, an instructor teaching undergraduates.

The word *undergraduates* enunciated with savage sarcasm.

But Walter did not suggest us meeting again, when he might have more time.

Emphatically then saying "Goodbye." Not lingering for my response but walking quickly away, briefcase thumping against his thigh. As years before, a far younger man, he'd climbed hurriedly into his battered old Ford and driven down Cayuga Avenue without a backward glance leaving M.'s younger sister G. forlorn and abandoned on the sidewalk in front of our house.

At that time, it might have been 1987, M. was alive, living in New York City. M. who knew nothing of our meeting, Walter and me. And if she'd never returned, to care for "Gigi," she might be alive now, this very day.

Walter, too, might be alive. Not in Hell.

Stricken, I watched Walter Lang flee, for the second time. A terrible urge came to me, to call after him. *Walter! Wait. I have so much more to tell you . . .*

Of course, I did not. I did not say a word, I did not even curse as a lanky-limbed young man collided with me, sending me stumbling and nearly falling on the steps with a glib apology over his shoulder: "Hey ma'am! Sor-ry."

45

The Stoic. Over the years Father has become a stoic. Now in his early eighties he still walks ramrod-straight, his white hair is thick and tufted, and his eyebrows have grown gnarled over melancholy pouched eyes. His skin is relatively unlined, for a man of his age, but appears to have thinned, and bleeds easily; his forearms and the backs of his hands are often bruised for he takes prescription medicines that "thin" his blood in the hope of preventing strokes.

He has ceased publicly lamenting the loss of Marguerite, as he has ceased complaining bitterly of the "shoddy" police investigation into her disappearance, that was allowed to "go cold" so soon. Though from time to time he speaks wistfully of Drummard. I have no idea why. Perhaps Drummard represents the last of Father's hope.

Well, the fraud is resting peacefully. With the others, hard-packed dirt beneath aged wooden beams from which cobwebs drift like filigree.

No, I am not sorry. Not in the least sorry, why should I be?

Ashes to ashes. Eye for an eye.

With some reluctance Father finally gave up his office on Main Street, for he was going there less frequently, as arthritis has stiffened his limbs. Still, Father is very busy with philanthropic work and with his financial investments, sometimes with gratifying results, I gather, and sometimes with not such gratifying results, depending upon the vicissitudes of the market, to which he is cheerfully indifferent—indeed, *stoic*.

Of the Fulmer family estate, I have only the dimmest sense. I know that, following the advice of his money managers, Father has "divested" certain stocks and real estate properties; it's my sense that his holdings have diminished somewhat, since a steep decline in 2008, but we never discuss such matters. Years ago Father established a trust to assure my financial well-being, if and when I find myself living alone in this large old house; there is said to be an equivalent trust established for Marguerite, should she ever return to claim it.

(Yes, relatives shake their heads over what they perceive to be Father's stubborn optimism, not realizing that it is a simply a stoic's way of *hedging his bets*.)

In recent years Father has, surprisingly, resumed the once-scorned habit of churchgoing, interrupted for decades after Mother's untimely death; Milton Fulmer has become a "pillar" of our local Anglican church, a familiar presence amid the company of Fulmer relatives he has grown to tolerate, and whom I avoid. Not often but sometimes, if I am in a perverse mood, I accompany Father on Sunday mornings for it can be gratifying to snub nosy relatives and neighbors; especially, I am pitiless in ignoring my callow cousin Denise who always casts quizzical/hopeful/ reproachful glances in my direction. In the Fulmer family pew beside me Father sits in silence, in melancholy repose, an unopened hymnal on his lap.

Once, at the conclusion of a particularly tedious service, Father glanced about us blinking as if uncertain of his surroundings, and murmured in my ear: "Remind me, please—why did your sister marry outside the church? *Did* she 'marry outside the church'?"

Stricken by this perplexing query I could only stammer: "I—I can't speak for Marguerite, Father. No one can."

Surely it's progress of a kind that Father rarely speaks of M. even on her birthday, or on the anniversary of her disappearance, but I know that he is thinking of her as his eyes soften with regret, sorrow.

At which time I reach out to squeeze Father's cool, thin hand, with its bruised and liver-spotted skin, which responds with an absent-minded sort of paternal affection; and there comes Father's startled glance at me—"Oh! Hello!"—as if, for the moment, he has forgotten who I am.

46

"Confession." In March 2013, a stunning surprise.

A sixty-six-year-old inmate serving two life sentences without parole at the Clinton Correctional Facility in Dannemora, New York, suddenly confessed to the Catholic chaplain at the prison that he'd killed "maybe a dozen" women in upstate New York in the years 1984 to 1991 of whom one, it seemed, might be *Marguerite Fulmer.*

Desperate to be forgiven for his sins, said to be suffering symptoms of syphilitic dementia, the notorious "Wolf's Head Lake Killer" (whom I will not dignify by naming), confessed to abducting, raping, and murdering women and girls in the Finger Lakes region of New York State as well as in the Adirondacks and Catskills; long a suspect in several of these cases, he'd been tried and convicted in just two.

Shown photographs of female victims in unsolved cases this person identified M. "unhesitatingly" according to detectives, saying "That's one of them"; though when closely questioned he was vague about the circumstances of where and when he'd encountered her, where he'd taken her in his car, and how he'd disposed of her body, at first claiming to have abducted her from a college campus in a city—maybe Buffalo, maybe Rochester. Later, he'd changed his story claiming that (possibly) he'd confused M. with another "blond-haired woman," insisting that he'd abducted M. from a "country road" and left her body in a lake nearby, weighed down with rocks.

Not a big lake. One of those—what d'you call them—little lakes: "Fingers . . ."

Asked if it was Cayuga Lake he'd frowned as if he had never heard the name before, then nodded vigorously.

Kai-yoo-gah. Yah.

Asked why he'd killed these women whom (evidently) he hadn't known the loathsome degenerate explained earnestly *It's the only way to get them to pay attention to you.*

In all, the Wolf's Head Lake Killer claimed to have stalked, abducted, raped, and murdered at least twelve women and girls—that he could remember. The prison

281

chaplain was convinced that he was telling the truth but detectives were skeptical. It isn't uncommon in cases like this, evidently, that a serial killer will exaggerate the number of his victims. He might be boasting, bragging to his listeners/hoping to impress them as well as "baring his soul." He might have killed some of the victims but not all of them; he might be appropriating murders committed by a cellmate or a buddy; he might be misremembering. Clearly this individual's brain was deteriorating, his memory corroding. He was reported to become "excitable" recalling isolated (and lurid) details of the killings but betrayed "confusion" about the identities of the victims.

He insisted yes, he'd killed them all. He spoke in a wistful cracked voice. He wept "like a sniveling baby." He was said to have lost a great deal of weight as if (possibly) he had a wasting illness like cancer. (State budgets for maximum security facilities do not allow for costly medical procedures like colonoscopies, nor should they; we taxpayers have enough to pay as it is.) Talking rapidly, stammering and coughing—"desperately anxious" to confess his sins before it was too late and he died, and went to Hell.

So many of them, I killed them all, Jesus forgive me. I buried them in water because it is soft and would not hurt. A pause.

Do you think He will?—Jesus? Forgive me?

A particularly stupid sort of pathos, as you might see on one of the coarser TV police programs. And disgusting.

Fortunately when the call came from Detective B___ (I have made no effort to remember any of their names) with the New York State Police, asking for Milton Fulmer, I was able to intervene and take the call, explaining that my father had more crucial business concerns than coming to the phone to speak with a stranger.

"But I am authorized to speak on Milton Fulmer's behalf," I explained. "I am fully cognizant of the 'missing persons' case pertaining to my sister Marguerite."

As a hippopotamus is equipped, with its thick rubbery skin, to deal with pestiferous insects, so I have become equipped to deal with preposterous developments in the "cold case" of Marguerite Fulmer. In a matter-of-fact voice I explained to Detective B___ that Father's health was excellent for a man of his age but still, Father was *not young*. Things can change rapidly in the elderly if there is a trauma, a shock. I was determined to protect Father from any shock.

And so I said firmly: unless this individual can lead police to an actual body, and unless there is forensic evidence linking that body to my sister Marguerite *definitively*, I had no intention of informing my father, or even of listening much longer to this drivel; for if the (syphilitic, demented) "serial killer" had not said anything specific enough that might be said to *prove* that he was my sister's murderer it was clearly all a ruse, and a waste of my time.

A startled pause! An audible intake of breath at the other end of the line.

Relatives of murder victims are more tractable and credulous, on the whole, than I, perhaps; no doubt, such pathetic souls are grateful for the most meager crumbs tossed at them by overpaid underachieving "professionals" in law enforcement, and it would never occur to them to doubt the nonsense they are gravely told, let alone articulate their skepticism so clearly over the phone as I did.

And then Detective B___ conceded, as if I had shown him my winning hand: "He says he has 'treasures' he'd taken from them—stockings, clothing—a 'fancy' watch 'all silver'—but he can't remember where the storage locker is. Unless we can locate these items you are correct, Ms. Fulmer, there's no way for us to know if he's telling the truth about your sister being one of his victims. He would have to lead us to the body, which he can't do, either. At this point we can only—"

Hanging up the phone. Hand trembling with indignation and fury.

For: I know that the "Wolf's Head Lake Killer" *was not* telling the truth, indeed everything he'd said was *drivel*.

47

Time to Bury. Entering M.'s room stealthily as if M. were present. My heavy footsteps made "lighter" through an act of will in case Lena is listening, below.

Peering through rain-lashed windows at the lake. *Had* M. drowned herself, in those fierce choppy waters? Not behind our house but elsewhere, miles away, where no one would think to search?

Quite possible. Plausible.

Such tales are still told, years later.

D'you remember that "heiress," disappeared, people say she drowned herself, love gone wrong . . .

For the ache of mystery is that we are compelled to solve it.

For the frustration of mystery is that we are not always able to solve it.

Entering M.'s room quietly. Inspecting the mirror that, despite Lena's efforts, is covered with a fine scrim of dust.

(But no: Lena has departed our household. Lena has not [yet] been replaced.)

Opening the closet door just so, so that it is reflected in the bureau mirror, two mirrors reflecting to infinity.

Terrible to see!—how the simplest reflection, in a reflection, vanishes into infinity.

The purpose of the visit is to inspect the Dior slip dress one final time.

Each occasion, over the years, carefully removing the dress, on its hanger, from its crammed-in position in the closet.

Silky white Dior slip dress light as filigree, light as lingerie. Lifting it to the light. Inhaling its aroma which, over the years, has become the aroma of time itself.

Today, bringing M.'s dress to the window, marveling at its lightness, silky white, lace-edged, with spaghetti straps, shocked to see that it has become faintly yellow, like old ivory, dried urine.

Not a gift from a lover. Not a *clue*. Never was.

Impulsively I think—*I will bury this too!*

Hard-packed earth, in the old, old section of the cellar where no one ever goes, where in the farthest corner you must make your way stoop-backed, or fall to your knees, to crawl.

48

April Dawn: the Summons. Wakened out of the deep pit of sleep by a furious tapping against the window beside my bed—icy rain, hailstones. Jolted awake in the twilit hour before dawn in despair of falling back to sleep.

In the (fine-spun) (icy-cold) bedsheets, in my threadbare flannel nightgown to my (icy) feet trying to comprehend *where, when is this?* For I have become very frightened.

April, yet so cold. The old house is rocked in the wind like a galleon on the high seas. Electricity flickers like a fibrillating heart—close to going *out.*

Bursts of swirling snow. Sudden April blizzard. At a high window I stare into the maelstrom of white. So alone!—lonely.

After an hour the snow begins to fall less heavily. Maybe we will be safe—Father and me. Like frost scraped from a window the sky clears in patches of brilliant blue.

Transfixed, unable to break away. Below my window is a sculpted sea of flawless white untouched by human or animal tracks.

And then I realize why I am at the window and why I am staring out into the sculpted-white sea for I am seeing her: my sister Marguerite in dark clothing poised and still against the white. Unmoving, as if she has been there for a long time, patient, waiting beneath the largest of the yew trees in our back lawn.

◆

My impulse is to step back quickly before M. sees me. But of course M. sees me.

So many times I have "seen" M. in twenty-two years, this is not such a shock, really. It should not have been a shock. It should not have frightened me so. But this morning M. doesn't turn away aloof and disdainful but continues to gaze at me lifting her eyes toward me as I stand in the window where I am not hidden but revealed.

My heart has begun to pound rapidly. I would like to call to Father, or to Lena, but my throat is tight, I cannot

289

speak. My fear is so great, it is a kind of peace, a tidal wave washing over me—*Now, it has happened. I have waited so many years.*

I have been faithful to M. I have not betrayed her.

When the storage locker rented in a fictitious name by the (so-called) Wolf's Head Lake Killer was located in a squalid Lake George strip mall and a battered suitcase crammed with women's things was discovered in it I did not fall for the ruse. I did not consent to meet with detectives and I did not "identify" certain of the items—indeed, "props"—they believed to have belonged to my sister: Longines wristwatch, hemp-woven handbag, pages torn from an artist's sketchbook.

I would not even consent to see the items. For I would not succumb to their blandishments.

The usual bewilderment at my decision. Disapproval, disgust among the relatives.

Georgene why on earth not—?

Just—*no.*

Refused to be a part of the farce. That a dim-witted lunatic had abducted, tortured, raped, and murdered my beautiful artist-heiress-sister—*no.*

Disposed of her body like trash—*no.*

Did not, and would not cooperate. *No.*

A suitcase said to be made of some cheaply synthetic material like vinyl crammed with tawdry "treasures."

Women's (torn, bloodied) underwear, rings, necklaces, several single shoes, several wristwatches of which one, no doubt the most beautiful and expensive, was believed to have once belonged to Marguerite Fulmer but they had no proof.

Father consented, of course. Father cooperated. Father conceded yes, the Longines watch with a (cracked) smoky face and very small numerals was M.'s, possibly. The hemp-woven bag which looked familiar to him, probably. Pages from an artist's sketchbook, miniature line drawings in pencil, definitely.

Other relatives perused the items including our cousin Denise who'd (allegedly) burst into tears at the sight of the watch.

("Allegedly"—since I was not there, and I did not observe.)

Now, Marguerite has come to *me*. No doubt in agreement with me, this farce has gone on long enough.

Let them think what they think. We know better.

Awaiting me, outside in the fresh-fallen snow. That look of exasperated patience as in clumsy haste I throw on clothes: bulky down jacket, corduroy trousers. Jam my feet into boots. Not M.'s elegant leather boots but my durable rubberized boots—large enough to accommodate my size-ten feet in thick woolen socks.

My hands are trembling badly. I fumble with the doorknob.

And suddenly I am outside, behind the house. It is windy, surprisingly cold. Wet air. Snow like clumps of white blossoms blown against my face.

My breath steams as I plead with M. standing thirty feet away calmly facing me: I am not young like you, I am forty-five years old. My joints are arthritic. My upper legs have become flaccid, my ankles are thick, swollen. In this cold wind my eyes leak the most ridiculous tears.

Bemused Marguerite watches me. The little teardrop scar on her left cheek glitters in the wet air. *Just come with me, Gigi. It's time.*

Turning to lead me. Along the familiar path. Grasses stiff as if frozen, creaking underfoot. There is the (cruel?) promise that I will be strong enough for the ordeal. I will not be tested beyond my strength.

Never before had I understood that *my life* is something living and fragile like the flame of a candle: in such wind, in danger of going *out.*

Unexpectedly, I am feeling exhilarated by the cold. Oxygen rushing to the brain can make you giddy. Though frightened I am also elated for at last I know where Marguerite *is.*

Outrageous to think M. could have been "buried" anywhere.

Outrageous to think that a dim-witted lunatic could have claimed my sister as *his*.

Feeling satisfaction, as when a lock is unbolted. That I alone of all the world have been granted this knowledge, withheld from others.

Now it is clear: Marguerite is *buried nowhere*. Not water, and not earth.

You silly Gigi! Come take my hand.

Making our way through the Fulmer property. Ancestral acres. Everywhere are fallen tree branches like amputated limbs. A juniper tree, split by lightning this past winter, or the winter before, has never been pruned but allowed to split further, sprawling on the ground like a kneeling girl, hair spread before her.

My boots sink inches deep in the hard-crusted snow, I am not nearly so graceful as M.

Already there are tracks in the snow, made by small animals, birds. Deer—you can see the sharp hooves.

But where are Marguerite's tracks?—I don't see them.

But I can see Marguerite clearly. It's crucial to follow her, never losing sight of the slender dark figure gliding light as shadow.

In the years since M. vanished from our lives upper Cayuga Avenue has lost its prestige. Neighboring houses have been sold, rezoned, and divided into apartments.

Fulmer relatives have quietly moved away, I am not sure where. For they never invite us.

Father and I live alone in the big old house. I'd forgotten—Lena died several years ago, we have been searching for her replacement ever since.

In the house, we live in just a few rooms. Most of the rooms are shut off. M.'s rooms remain untouched, awaiting her return.

Rarely do I step inside M.'s room any longer for I have memorized it entirely. The mirror on the back of the closet door, now kept closed. If I position myself correctly I can see, through this mirror, the mirror on the bureau; but the mirror on the bureau reflects nothing any longer for we have all departed.

In the closets M.'s beautiful clothes are intact, I suppose. Except for moth holes in woolen things. Camel's-hair coat, cashmere sweaters. Perhaps mice have built little nests on the shelves. Open a closet door, it will look as if M.'s expensive shoes have been cavorting together on the floor.

No, I didn't know: what the mammograms revealed. *If* the mammograms revealed anything out of the ordinary.

How would *I know*?—M. did not confide in G.

Not a *clue*, I don't think. Though (possibly) among M.'s things which I'd hurriedly thrown out were related documents, printouts of medical tests, not unlike Mother's myriad tests, no way to know this, pointless to speculate that my sister might have had a diagnosis that frightened her; that my sister might have had months of struggle; or only a few months to live.

Not clues. I retract them.

◆

Come, Gigi! Forget that.

We are finished with all that—bodies . . .

At the top of the incline M. has paused, waiting for me. Strange that M.'s breath doesn't steam even faintly while my breath is a series of steaming pants dissipating at once in the cold wet air.

Almost without knowing it we have crossed over into the no-man's-land owned by Aurora Township. Here are shattered trees, underbrush, litter. Shocking to see, near Drumlin Road, that people have been using this land as a common *dump*. When did this begin? What sort of slovenly citizens toss out broken toilets, filthy mattresses, wrecked bicycles, ravaged tires?—I am sorry that M. has to see this.

Perhaps for this reason M. leads me on an alternate path, away from the dump and through a stand of tall, ravaged oaks and yews, where snow is deeper, no one is likely to intrude.

295

My lungs ache! I am feeling how delicious it would be, to lie down in the fresh snow. To make a little nest for myself beneath yew limbs heavy with snow like wings.

Such loneliness, I am feeling now. I have not realized until now.

As M. walks resolutely ahead. I am frantic not to lose her. For I am so, so lonely.

Has this been my life? Since M.? Since the fear of M., leaving us.

Over the long upstate New York winter I have been unwell. My blood pressure is high, my eardrums feel as if they might burst. *I am not what people think. Tough as a hippo, wit like a whip.*

Only you know, dear sister forgive me.

Oh, why does M. walk so quickly, knowing that I can barely keep up! If only she would wait for me. Take my hand. She'd hugged me, when we were girls. *Why are you crying, silly Gigi!*

Slip-sliding in the icy snow. If I fall on this hill my leg will twist beneath me. If I fall heavily something will crack in my ribcage. A sharp rib bone, penetrating the wall of the heart.

I will lie very still, I will make a little nest for myself in the snow. The freezing wind will blow over me sparing me. Bones creaking about me like the ribs of an old seafaring ship and anger seeping out of my heart that beats slower, slower.

Slow-dawning sun, a cold blue eye opening overhead with excruciating precision.

Dear sister, wait! I am almost there.